IT'S THE BASS PLAYER!

Cabot Barden

PublishAmerica
Baltimore

© 2011 by Cabot Barden.
All rights reserved. No part of this book may be reproduced, stored in a retrieval system or transmitted in any form or by any means without the prior written permission of the publishers, except by a reviewer who may quote brief passages in a review to be printed in a newspaper, magazine or journal.

First printing

All characters in this book are fictitious, and any resemblance to real persons, living or dead, is coincidental.

PublishAmerica has allowed this work to remain exactly as the author intended, verbatim, without editorial input.

Hardcover 978-1-4560-5354-3
Softcover 978-1-4560-5353-6
PUBLISHED BY PUBLISHAMERICA, LLLP
www.publishamerica.com
Baltimore

Printed in the United States of America

This book is dedicated to my good friend, Charlie, who has alzheimers.

CHAPTER 1

He climbed the hill once again to see his friends who lived in the green house at the end of the street where most of the well-to-do folks lived. As he walked the path through the woods, he dreamed of someday living in a "big fine home in a ritzy neighborhood". Even though Toby lived in a fairly nice neighborhood of brick houses and manicured lawns, he wanted more than this. He hadn't brought his swimming trunks with him for the Gables' pool, because his trunks were kept at Corey's house, since the only place that Toby Martin went swimming that summer was at the Gable's house. Toby and Corey had spent the week before draining, cleaning, and painting the Gables' in-the-ground concrete pool. They couldn't get help from Corey's or Toby's brothers, due to the common opinion that cleaning it was a lost cause.

"Boy. Did we show them. We proved them wrong." thought Toby.

His thoughts turned to cooling his body in the chlorinated water, and diving off the board into the twelve foot deep pool. His feet merrily trodded along the path up the side of the hill through the woods. As he reached the top of the hill, the path came out into Corey Gable's backyard. He could see that Corey's older brother, John, had been cutting the grass earlier that morning. The freshly cut grass was still green. Toby quickly walked across the patio to the living room door. He knocked lightly.

"Come on in." came Corey's voice. Toby went on in. "Ready for that nice cool water?" Corey asked cheerfully.

Toby replied, "I noticed on y'all's thermometer out there that it's only 98 degrees in the shade. It feels so good in this air conditioning. I kinda hate to go back out. Is anybody else going swimming this morning?"

"Nah. John went to town with mom." answered Corey.

Toby said, "Well. Looks like the pool is ours for now. I'll go change and we'll hit it."

"All right!" yelled Corey. "Oh yeah. Have you heard anything from Fred about any bookings?"

"Not yet." called Toby from the bathroom. "You know we've still got one more weekend at the American Legion behind the Armory."

"Yeah." said Corey disgustedly. "I wish we could get some bookings playing for people our age, instead of a bunch of beer bottle throwing old drunks. Yaahoo!" said Corey sarcastically.

"Yeah. It's the same thing every year. After football season and the after game parties, the only places to play around here are the honky tonk dives. But Fred did say he was going to try to get that agent out of Tuscaloosa to book us." said Toby as he walked back into the living room in his swimming trunks. "Last one in the pool is a Cleep!"

They raced to the pool and jumped in.

Fred Litton was nervously drumming his fingers on the end table as he sat waiting for the person at the other end of the phone call to answer. On the fifth ring a sexy southern female voice answered, "Good mawnin. Markus Attractions."

"Let me speak to someone in charge of band bookings please." Fred inquired anxiously. "Are you needin' a band foh a pahty suh?" the voice asked.

IT'S THE BASS PLAYER!

"No ma'am. I play in a band, and I'd like to see if my group can get a couple of bookings." answered Fred.

"One moment and I'll connect you to Mr. Wadkins." she said. Ten seconds later a very deep voice answered,

"This is Johnny Wadkins. What can I do you for?" Fred cleared his throat and started, "Mr. Wadkins, this is Fred Litton in Chalaka. I've got a band called Common Faith, and we're needin' some bookings."

The deep voice asked, "Well. What kind of music do you guys play?"

"We play top forty sir." replied Fred.

"Can the "sir" crap. Just call me Johnny. What kind of top forty? Country, rock, or what?"

"Well sir, ah, Johnny, we do mostly rock, pop, and easy listening. We've got a lead guitarist, bass player, keyboard man, drummer, lead vocalist, and female vocalist." "That's perfect for the bookings I've got lined up. When could your band start playing?" Fred answered, "We've got one more weekend at a local American Legion that's coming up, but after that we're pretty much open."

"Good. I've got a booking in Columbus Mississippi at an Air Force Base for two Nights three weekends from now. I'll put your group down for that. Meanwhile, you can send me your promo shots, some business cards, and a song list."

"Promo shots?" Fred stuttered.

Johnny said, "Yeah. you can get them to me anytime between now and Wednesday week. "Oh. Right. We'll have them to you just as quick as we can." Fred answered as he gritted his teeth.

Johnny said, "Good. I'll go ahead and get the contracts to you to sign. You can get them back to me as soon as possible. I'm looking forward to doing business with you. Let my secretary get your name, phone number, and the other information, so I'll know where to send the contracts."

"Great! I'm looking forward to doing business with you too. Goodbye Mr., ah, Johnny." smiled Fred.

"Bye Fred Litton. Was it?"

"Yes sir." After giving the secretary the information, Fred hung up the phone and sat there thinking, "We finally got a booking agent that WILL book us!"

Fred's mother, Verna, walked into the den where Fred was sitting and said, "Well Did you get hold of that booking agent you was trying to reach?"

Fred looked up and said, "Yes ma'am. And even better, I believe I got us a booking three weeks from now. I've got to get things organized. But where do I start? I've got a little less than two weeks to get everybody together for pictures and practice, and maybe I'd better round up Toby and Corey first. I'll bet Toby would probably be at Corey's in the pool right now. I'll just go up there and see."

"All right hon. But don't be late for supper." Mrs. Litton called out as Fred went out the door.

Fred walked out the door of his mother's house on the Southside of town, and got into his nineteen sixty eight GTO. His hometown of Chalaka wasn't anything near the size of Birmingham, but it wasn't so small that everyone knew everyone else's business either. It was definitely no Mayberry, and there were no Andy Griffith characters on the police force. The population was about thirteen thousand. The downtown area had the businesses lined up and down the main streets of Norton and Broadway. It also had three shopping centers, which accommodated several department stores, grocery stores, and various what-not shops. On the way to Corey's, Fred drove by the Frosty Inn. The hang out for all the kids that

IT'S THE BASS PLAYER!

went to the city school. He and his best friends that he grew up with always hung out at the Frosty Inn on the weekends when there was nothing else to do. If you played football for Chalaka High School, you hung out at the Frosty. The kids that went to the county school that was literally across the tracks from the city school, always hung out at the Dairy Queen, which was about a block from the Frosty Inn. Fred was an alumnus of Chalaka High School. He was right guard on the football team the year before. His team had won the state 3-A championship his senior year. Because of this he had gotten a scholarship to play football at one of the colleges in the state. Some of his peers liked to poke fun at him occasionally because of his seldom awkwardness at the wrong moment. Like the night he graduated. Coming off the stage after receiving his diploma, he tripped on his graduation gown and almost landed in the middle of some girl's lap that played in the high school band that was sitting at the foot of the stairs. The one remark that he could live without hearing again was, "Atta boy Fred!". He was the right size for a football player, and looked the part of the clean cut, all-American type. Fred, Toby, and Corey were all different in appearance. But they had a common bond between them. They were like the three Musketeers. There was a common faith in their friendship, which fit the name of their band, the Common Faith. Where Fred was a tall six feet three inches, light complected, with light brown hair, Toby was a stocky five feet eight inches, dark complected, and dark brown hair. Corey was very thin, wirey and limber, fair complected, and black curly hair. He stood six feet tall in his size twelve shoes. Corey was the clown of the trio. He had the kind of personality that almost everyone liked when they met him. Toby was a cutup in his own right as well. Fred could get goofy at times too, but he was more prone to be "down to earth" most of the time.

Fred pulled up in the driveway at the Gables' house. He got out and walked around to the side yard where the pool was, following the noise from people playing in the pool. Toby, Corey, Corey's brother, John, and their neighbor, Brenda were playing chicken. A game where one person sits on another's shoulders in the water, and tries to knock down another couple doing the same. Corey and Toby were engaged in toppling Brenda off John's shoulders.

"All right! Dat's right! We bad!" yelled Toby.

"Ugh! You guys don't play fair." gurgled a half drowned Brenda. "Next time I ride Toby's shoulders and John rides Corey."

"Hey! What are you trying to do? John weighs twice as much as me! He'll break my back." argued Corey.

"That's the general idea." Brenda said with an evil grin.

Toby was the first to notice Fred standing at the fence. "Hey Fred. Got your shorts on? Come on in! The water's nice and cool."

"Nah. I don't have time. For that matter, neither do you guys." answered Fred.

"Guys?" asked Brenda with a pout.

Fred continued, "I got hold of the agent in Tuscaloosa and guess what? We got a booking. But we've got one problem. He wants pictures, a business card, and a songlist." "We don't have any of that, except maybe the songlist." Toby replied.

"Right. That's why we've got to get it done now. Today. Corey, I'm gonna use your phone to call Mann's photography studio." stated Fred.

"Sure. Go on in. Mom's decent." Corey said as he was getting out of the pool. "Come on Tobe. Let's get with it!"

"Right you are my friend." replied Toby excitedly.

"Aren't you gonna let me ride on your shoulders?" asked Brenda faking a hurt look. Toby smiled and said, "You know

IT'S THE BASS PLAYER!

me. When it comes to music, it's always business before pleasure."

"The trouble is, your business IS your pleasure, when it comes to music." whimpered Brenda playfully.

"She's got ya there Tobe." chuckled John.

"Touche." grinned Toby. As Toby walked into the kitchen, Fred was hanging up the phone. "You probably need to call Ben and Paul. And especially Donna. We sure can't make pictures without her. said Toby.

"I'm two steps ahead of ya Tobe." smiled Fred. "The picture session is in the morning, and I've already called Ben and Paul. I was just fixin' to call Donna."

"Man. With a blonde bombshell like her in the picture, we're bound to get bookings up to our armpits." smiled Corey.

"Yeah. When you look at her, just think of dollar signs all over that good lookin body." grinned Fred.

"Just remember about the jinx though." warned Corey soberly.

"What jinx?" from Fred.

"You know? The one about taking pictures. Every time we have a picture made of the group, somebody always quits."

"Not this time." said Fred. "I've got a contract coming that everyone has to sign. I figure as long as I can get bookings through Markus Attractions, and keep the contracts coming, nobody would dare quit."

"I hope you're right." said Toby as he walked toward the bathroom to change. "I'll be back in a minute." he called over his shoulder. Toby walked into the hallway and saw that the bathroom door was closed. He decided to knock, since the door was closed and would not lock.

A voice from within said, "Come on in Toby."

Toby thought John must be in there. He opened the door, walked in, closing the door behind him, looked up and said, "Hey John. Guess…what?"

He stopped dead in his tracks. His body froze in motion. He thought his eyeballs were going to pop out of their sockets. He felt his heart suddenly pounding in his chest. His cheeks flushed. His ears felt like they were going to pop. He felt a sensation stirring in him he couldn't control. There, standing in front of him was the first actual topless teenage girl he had ever seen. Brenda was leaning against the sink counter top with one hand, and the other propped on her hip. Her brown eyes twinkling with mischief.

"I knew you were coming so I baked a cheesecake." she said with a wolfish smile. "How about it big boy?"

By this time Toby was a glorious crimson red. His whole body was trembling. He knew that Corey's mom, Gladys, was in the house. He tried to say something that made sense. "Uh. Uh. I uh." was all that came out.

"What's a matter? Kitty cat got your tongue?" taunted Brenda.

"God! If I get caught like this, it'll ruin everything." he thought.

He was right. If he got caught like this, in that room with Brenda halfway in the flesh, Gladys would tell him to never set foot in the Gable house again. Corey would have to quit the band and Toby could never come up and go swimming again.

"Wait a minute." he thought, "That's it!"

He reached behind him and grabbed the doorknob.

With a crimson smile he said, "I forgot something out at the pool. Bye."

He turned and quickly exited, closing the door behind him. He ran through the living room, out the door, across the patio, and dove back in the pool, hearing loud laughter from the bathroom as he ran.

CHAPTER 2

The Picture Session

"Are we all here?" asked Fred.

"Yeah. Toby and Donna just pulled up out front in their cars."answered Corey.

"Hey Corey. What's up with Toby?"

"What do ya mean Fred?"

"Well. I don't know. He's been acting a little strange since yesterday at the pool." stated Fred.

"Yeah. I noticed it too Fred, when I went back out to the pool to get my towel. You know? When you were calling Donna, and Toby had gotten back in the pool. I asked him why he got back in, when we had so much to do, and he mumbled something about his nineteen year old eyes had lost their virginity. He must have found the Playboy calendar under John's bed, that nobody's supposed to know about."

"You mean John has a Playboy calendar?" asked a surprised Fred.

"Oops. I wasn't supposed to say that." chuckled Corey.

"Hey guys. Is Donna here yet?" asked Toby as he walked up.

"Right here." came a very feminine voice from behind him.

"Whooeee! You look like a million bucks!" exclaimed Paul Thornton, the band's keyboard man.

"Thank you. I do try. Especially when I'm going to be surrounded by some good looking boys." smiled Donna with that knowing look that a cat gets when she's trapped a mouse. "Then let's go do this thing." grinned Fred.

Ten minutes later the six of them were going through different poses that the cameraman had set up for the group. With a background of a Peace poster, a picture of Tiny Tim, and a collage of colors poster, they smiled away under the bright lights. They posed and grinned while the camera shutters snapped and the automatic advance drive in the camera whirred.

One hour later Ben Regis, the lead singer for the group, was saying, "Man. I'm glad that's over with. I hate picture sessions."

"Well what are you gonna do when we become famous? They'll be snappin' our pictures all the time then." smiled Corey.

"Dream on Corey. Cause that's all you're doin' is dreamin'. Stuff like that only happens in the movies. Nobody makes it big in the music business on just their talent, unless they got money to burn. And even then, they have to know the right people. And who do WE know in this half-horse town?" groused Ben.

"Oh. Let him dream Ben. After all, that's where all of our plans in life come from." stated Fred.

"Fred's right. Where would we be without our dreams?" asked Toby.

"Well if you gentlemen will excuse me, I've got to go home and get ready for majorette practice at my old alma mater." purred Donna as she walked toward the front door of the studio. "Let me know how the pictures turn out."

"Wait a minute. You've been out of high school since May. You're not a majorette anymore." stated Fred.

"I know that." Donna smiled. I just figured the new girls could use some pointers from a pro." With that, she turned and

IT'S THE BASS PLAYER!

swiveled her hips in an exaggerated way, like she was marching in a parade, as she walked out the door.

After she went out, Paul said wistfully, "Woo woo! Man! I wish I had a swing like that in my backyard."

"Forget it. She's hung up on some jock from the cow college." grimaced Fred.

"Yeah. I remember when she dumped you, Fred, because she thought football jocks were air heads. Now look who she's hot after. Mr. "Most valuable player in the SEC". Tell me women ain't weird." said Toby as he squinched up his nose.

"Well. One thing's for sure. If her supposed heart throb is ninety miles away, he sure can't keep tabs on her from way down there, if she decides to fool around with somebody back here at home." asserted Corey.

"Well. I don't really care, so let's drop the subject. Okay? Besides, what she does is her business as long as it doesn't effect the band." bantered Fred

. Toby and Corey could tell that Donna was still a sore subject for Fred, so they said no more about it.

"Well, I'll see you guys at the war zone." Ben said with a twinkle in his eye.

"The what?" asked Fred.

"You know. The American Legion Post, where, if you don't have a knife or gun when you come in the door, they issue you one." smiled Ben.

"He means the club where his buddy hangs out." snickered Corey.

"What buddy?" asked a puzzled Ben.

"You know? The one you punched his lights out for kissing you on the cheek when you thought he was just requesting a song?" laughed Toby.

"Yeah. And if he does it again, I'll break his freakin' neck!" snarled Ben.

They were all laughing so hard by then, there wasn't a dry eye among them, except for Ben, who finally just grinned mischievously.

"The pictures will be…ready…Thursday." stated a quite puzzled photographer, who had just walked into a room full of teary-eyed hysterical boys.

Fred managed to thank the man and tell him he'd be back Thursday to pick up the pictures.

CHAPTER

The Dive and the Fight

Toby and Corey sat in the parking lot of the American Legion Post that next Saturday evening, waiting for Fred, in Toby's nineteen sixty Pontiac Star Chief, which was affectionately known as the blue goose. His dad had bought the car new in nineteen sixty, and since Toby's mom had bought her a nineteen sixty eight Pontiac Le Mans, the Blue Goose had been given to Toby to drive. Most of the guys he knew had nicknames for their cars. Corey's brother, John, had an old nineteen sixty four Ford Fairlane four door they called the black bomb, because of the loud muffler on it. It wasn't fast, just loud. Corey had borrowed it to come play. They had been playing at the American Legion Post for about a month and a half on Saturday nights. Only four of the members played there though. Paul, the keyboard man, wouldn't play there because there wasn't enough pay for five guys to split and really make anything. Donna didn't want to go there because she said it was too rough for a lady. The rest of the guys agreed that she didn't need to be in that dump. So that left Fred on guitar and backup vocals, Ben on rhythm guitar and lead vocals, Corey on drums, and Toby on bass and back up vocals. Mostly all that hung out at this place was older people who were cheating on their spouses, or messing with someone else who was cheating on theirs. Most of the women in the place couldn't even attract flies anymore, as Ben put it.

"Fred just pulled up. Let's see if he got the pictures. Maybe got extra prints, so we can have a copy too." said Corey.

"Yeah. You should've done the crab in one of 'em." grinned Toby.

"Sorry guys. But the only pictures I got I sent them on to the agent." muttered Fred as he walked up.

"Oh well. What about the business cards? Did you get those?" asked Toby.

"Oh yeah. I've got a bunch of those. Here." answered Fred as he passed out a handful of cards to Corey and Toby.

"Thanks. Hey! Wait a minute. It only has your name and number on it with the name of the band. What about the rest of us? Don't we count in this band too?" asked Corey.

"You think there'd be any room left on the card for the name of the band if I put EVRYBODY'S name on here? Besides guys, I'll be the one handling the bookings. That is, unless one of you two crazies want to handle 'em." replied Fred.

"No thanks. I'd rather just worry about my performance on stage." vollied Corey.

"What stage? Oh.you mean that corner of the room that we play in that dump." Toby jestured toward the dilapidated building behind him.

"Gee guys. Think of the money. And besides, this is probably our last weekend here. Especially since we got this booking in Mississippi." smiled Fred.

"By the way Fred, how much money are we talking on this booking coming up?" asked Toby.

"Three hundred a night for Friday and Saturday. And it's two different clubs on base. Friday night is the Officers' club and Saturday night is the Servicemens' club." answered Fred.

"Wow! That's the most money we've made in one weekend." exuded Corey.

IT'S THE BASS PLAYER!

"Yeah. But don't forget expenses. We'll have to rent a trailer, we gotta eat, have a place to sleep Friday night, and who knows what else?" droned Fred.

"We'll still come out better than playing here. Anything beats playing here." whined Corey. "You gonna tell what's-his-face we're not coming back?"

Fred smiled, "You mean Mr. "I own this club" Ensign? Are you kidding? Why tell him anything? We'll just pack up tonight, take our money and leave. He doesn't like the music we play anyway. He thinks Creedence Clearwater is hard rock." snickered Fred.

"Yeah. What a bumpkin!" Laughed Toby. "Well. I see Ben's finally here. Let's get set up and get a sound check on the P.A."

They set up their equipment in the corner of the old block building in the largest room, where the tile wasn't buckling and coming up off the floor. As they set up, Toby noticed there was one booth toward the back of the room where someone was laying there snoring very loudly.

"Hey. I wonder if he's a leftover from last weekend?" he asked.

"Probably. These old drunks that come in here drink enough to pickle them for the next hundred years." called Fred over his Shoulder, as he set up his Sunn one hundred watt guitar amplifier, with speaker cabinet containing two fifteen inch speakers. Then he got his Gretsch Country Gentleman electric guitar out and started tuning it up. It was a bright orange color. Toby always complained about the strings being too high off the neck for him to play, but Fred had no trouble playing it because he was used to playing it.

Toby got out his Audition bass guitar, that was bought at Woolworth's. At that time, it was all he could afford to buy for a bass guitar. When he bought it, it only had 3 strings on it, so Toby had to buy a new set of strings to put on it. It sounded pretty good for a cheap musical instrument that it was. He plugged it into his Plush bass guitar amplifier, with one hundred watts of power, and a speaker cabinet with two fifteen inch bass speakers in it. In those days, the bigger the amplifier, the more impressive you were as a rock musician.

"I still say that amplifier looks more like a piece of furniture, with all that rolled and pleated vinyl on it. When you gonna finish that bass guitar, Tobe? You've got all the paint sanded off. It looks kinda naked to me." quipped Corey.

"Don't say naked." rasped Toby.

"Okay. Okay. Excuse me. Are you sure you're all right, Tobe?" asked Corey hesitantly. "Yeah. I'm fine. Just had a lousy day. That's all. Sorry. Didn't mean to snap at ya." apologized Toby.

Three hours later, the band was into it's third forty five minute set, coming up on their third fifteen minute break, when Toby noticed in the back of this room full of old nasty drunk white men and women, there was something totally out of place. In a corner booth sat a black man and his nicely dressed date. He had a Legionaire's cap parked neatly on his well groomed head. The couple was dressed very nicely and conservatively, which made them stand out even more so in this dive full of overalled nasty people. Toby watched as the black man got up and went to the bar. No sooner had he left than two old inebriated men started taunting and badgering his date.

They kept telling her to "Get up and do some of them African dances that black folks was doin' these days or they'd throw her out."

To which she jumped up, pushed her way past them, and ran out the door. Meanwhile, there had been some noises

IT'S THE BASS PLAYER!

coming from the doorway that went into the bar, that sounded like a fight going on. The Common Faith finished their last song of the third set, and took a break. Toby and Fred headed for the restroom to relieve themselves. Toby walked in first and caught a glimpse of something red on the grey concrete floor in the men's room. It was a trail of red coming from the door outside leading into the shower stall. Toby walked over and cautiously pulled the shower curtain back. His eyes went wide at the sight they beheld. There was the black man, who had been sitting in his booth earlier. His face was ashen. His shirt torn almost off. His face, arm, and torso bleeding down his slacks and onto the shower stall tiled floor.

"Hey. You'd better get to the hospital before you bleed to death." exclaimed Toby in a low voice. The black man motioned for Toby to be quiet.

"Hey. You all right in there Toby? You didn't get it stuck in the toilet again. Did ya?" Called Fred from outside the door.

"Git me outa heyah man." begged the black man. "Dey tried to kill me."

"Okay. Okay. Just let me tell my buddy to make sure the coast is clear." Toby said, trying to calm the man.

"Hey. No. I didn't believe the Ku Klux hung out up heyah. My buddies tried to warn me. Just git me outa heyah."

"It's allright." promised Toby. "Trust me. Here. Wrap this towel around your arm. It'll help stop the bleeding. Just stay put. I'll be right back."

Toby stuck his head out the door and told Fred to see if the coast was clear and told him why. Fred looked around the room. Only two boothes were occupied by couples. A couple more had some drunks passed out in them.

Fred poked his head back in the restroom and said, "Okay. Go for it!"

The black man didn't need anymore prompting. He was out the door and across the dance floor in seconds. He was out the front door of the building even quicker. Toby and Fred slowly walked back up to the corner their equipment was set up in.

"I hope he makes it to the hospital okay." Fred said to no one in particular.

He and Toby knew that if they got caught helping this man by any of the rednecks who cut him up, that he and Toby would get a lot worse treatment. Although he and Toby could have held their own in a fistfight, these old codgers carried guns and knives. At that moment, two loud shots were heard right outside the entrance door to the club. A large hole splintered in the door.

"Jesus! Duck!" yelled Fred, as he and Toby hit the floor on their stomachs.

They crawled over behind their amps, where they found Corey crouched down behind his drums.

"What in the hell is goin' on?" squealed Corey.

"You said it right when you said hell, Corey, cause this is it." rasped Toby.

They stayed put for about another ten minutes.

"Hey. You can come out now. They took the black guy to the hospital, and arrested the guys that were doing the shooting." said Ben, as he walked up to the make-shift stage. "Who are they?" asked a very irritated Fred.

"The police of course. You were expecting the cavalry or somethin'?" retorted Ben."Whew! I'm glad that's over with." groaned Corey.

"This place should be burned to the ground." growled Toby.

"Why? All these old drunks would just find another sleaze hole to crawl in." answered Ben.

IT'S THE BASS PLAYER!

"Let's finish this last set and go home." declared Fred.

"Amen to that. I'm glad we won't be coming back here anymore." shuddered Toby.

They played the last set without interruption. They packed up their equipment and loaded it in their cars, except for Fred, who was busy collecting their pay for the night, from the man behind the bar, who ran the club.

"You boys is gonna have to learn more country. I mean real country, like Hank Williams and Ernest Tubb." the old geezer said. "If you don't learn San Antonio Rose, I'm gonna cut yore throat boy."

"Yes sir. We'll do our best." grimaced Fred.

"Come on Fred. We're loaded up and ready to go." called Toby from the door.

Fred walked out the door with Toby.

"You know what that old bag of dirt said? If I didn't learn San Antonio Rose he was gonna cut my throat." Fred hoarsely whispered.

Toby started singing, "And I was honky tonkin', honky tonkin'. Dadoo dadoo. Honky tonkin', honky tonkin'. Dadoo dadoo. Honky tonkin', honky tonkin'. What a life, what a life, what a life."

"I think all this funky air in this joint has gotten to your brain Tobe." grinned Fred, as they came out into the parking lot.

Toby said, "One thing's for sure. After what you and I saw that they did to that black guy, I don't ever want to come back in this hell hole again. They could just as well decide to cut us up simply because they don't like our music."

Fred frowned, "You're right about that Tobe. We won't be back here ever."

The four guys received their pay, said goodnight, and left. Corey and Ben agreed with Fred And Toby about not playing at this place again.

Toby pulled into his driveway at the house. He opened the car door and trudged up the sidewalk to the front door. He didn't realize how bone-tired he was until he stepped in the door to the house. His mother, Louise, was working third shift in the emergency room at the local hospital. She had worked there since after Toby was born. She had told him several times that she didn't want to see him come in on a stretcher, because of some old drunk went crazy in that pest hole Toby had been playing at. After this night, he knew she was justified in what she felt. Toby's brother, Mark, was sitting on the couch, watching a hokey horror show called "Dead Earnest" on channel seventeen. He was about half asleep.

"How'd it go?" yawned Mark.

"Pretty bad. You don't wanna know." Toby yawned back.

"That bad. Huh?" asked Mark.

"Yup. I'm glad you weren't there". said Toby. "See you in the morning."

Toby laid down to get some sleep in what was left of the night. It was two thirty in the morning and Toby's body knew it all too well. Yet his mind would not slow down. It was still churning over the events of the previous week. The picture session, the booking agent booking them in a club in Mississippi, and the embarrassing scene in the bathroom at Corey's. The image of the black man that had been cut up at the club went through his mind and he shuddered. It was hard to imagine that people could hate each other so much just because of the color of their skin. He figured that some people had an easier time hating other people than loving them or just tolerating them. He never knew when, but sleep finally found him.

CHAPTER 4

The Cave

His name was Clyde, but everyone called him Billy. He was a very out going athletic type with a strong competitive attitude. He was never overbearing in getting his way with his friends though. Toby's first impression of Billy was "The perfect gentleman". A guy that you just instantly like.

"Did you bring a flashlight, Bill?" asked Toby, as they started across Mr. Hightower's pasture.

"Yeah. Check out what else is in my backpack."

"Wow. You've got cherry bombs and M-80s." chirped Corey.

"What are you gonna do? Start a war?" smiled Toby.

"Nah. I just thought I'd see what it sounds like when I set one off in the caves." replied Billy.

"Hey man. That's liable to cause the roof to fall in." cautioned Toby. "I'm not going to be down there when you set one off."

"Tobe, I thought you knew me better than that. I'm gonna wait till we come back out, then throw some down in the entrance. And if I just happen to see a fresh cow patty that might be interesting to blow up, I might just do that. You know. The kind that's freshly laid on a fireant bed?" Billy reassured Toby.

It was a good mile and a half from the gate in Fairmont across Mr. Hightower's pasture to the hill where the old abandoned mines were. That's where they were headed. To explore the old mines. The mines had been dug out back in the early nineteen hundreds. No one was sure what exactly was dug out of the ground there. Some speculated Gold and others thought it was just an old slag mine. Slag was used in making steel in the early nineteen hundreds.

"Yeah. But don't get too close when it goes off, cause we don't want to smell cow crap on you all the way back." chuckled Toby.

The Tallasahatchee Creek ran length wise through the center of the pasture. The boys had fished on this creek since Toby and Billy were thirteen. The caves were located almost at the top of the hill at the far end of the pasture. The climb to the top of the hill from the pasture in some places was almost straight up on the well worn path, which meandered up the hill. The lower entrance was smaller. It was about two hundred yards below the larger main entrance, which was almost at the top of the hill. Water from an underground stream stood about three feet deep on the left side of the entrance to the smaller cave. The temperature in this one was a constant forty five degrees year round. Up and to the right in the lower cave was a passage which was just large enough for a well sized man to fit through. This led to a three foot wide tunnel, which went up and over a thirty foot mound of rock. The tunnel was eight feet in height. The upper cave was seventy feet in diameter at the mouth. Directly across from the upper entrance was an old wagon trail, which led down the backside of the mountain. Billy, Corey, Toby, and Toby's brother, Donald, climbed to the top of the hill, to the large cave entrance. It was a typical summer day in Alabama. About ninety two degrees in the shade. It was a lot cooler in the cave. As they climbed down the steep side of the cave entrance, Toby noticed a black, charred

IT'S THE BASS PLAYER!

place on top of one of the large gray rocks which were strode all over the floor of the cave.

"I see someone camped out down here recently." he said.

The first room was about fifty feet in height and fifty feet across. At the lower end of this first room were two tunnels going off to the left and right approximately ten feet in height. The tunnel on the right curved back up into another chamber that was half the size of the first one. There was no light in this chamber, except what little filtered in from the first chamber, so the boys turned on their flashlights.

"Look. The walls are glowing." exclaimed Corey.

The walls shimmered when the flashlights danced over them. Toby reached out and felt of the slimy substance on the wall. It felt gooey to the touch.

"It's algae with moisture all over it." he said.

"Let me see." said Billy.

He smeared his fingers across the shimmering slime, turned and smeared it on Corey's shirt.

"Eeewwww! It's the green slime!" he squealed in mock fear."Corey's been attacked by the ominous radioactive slime monster."

"Oh no!" screamed Corey. It's transforming me into another creature!"

With that, Corey fell on the cave floor and writhed and wriggled into a squatting position. "Oh no. He's turning into Corey the Crab!" laughed Donald.

Corey had put his elbows behind his knees, with his palms on the floor. He then picked up his legs and proceeded to walk on his hands from side to side. He growled ominously, "Hey you. I'm from outa town! Don't hang around if I'm unsanitary."

All four of them started laughing until their sides hurt. They came back into the first chamber. At the bottom of the back wall of this chamber was a three foot square hole, behind which was another chamber, two thirds as large as the first one.

"There's no way we can go down this way." said Donald.

He was right. The floor behind the three foot hole dropped away at an eighty five degree angle. It was covered with loose rock and dirt. At the bottom of the inclined floor was another three foot hole filled with water.

"I wonder if there are any blind salamandars in that?" pointed Billy at the hole filled with water. "I hear they're pretty common in underground streams."

"Hey y'all. Here's another way down." called Corey from the room off to the left.

Billy, Toby and Donald walked over. There was a six by three foot hole cut in the far corner of this small room. There was cool air flowing up out of this hole.

"Hey. Maybe there's a tunnel leading to the smaller cave down this way." Donald said. "Come on."

They climbed down a two foot drop to the downward sloping floor. Old rotted wooden beams that had fallen long ago were evident in several places on the floor. The angle here was about thirty degrees on the floor.

"Let's go down and get a closer look at that hole full of water." said Billy.

They walked down to the bottom of the room, where the hole filled with water was.

"I wonder how deep this thing went before it flooded?" wondered Corey.

"It looks like there was another room down there. The hole is exactly the same size as the one up there, that connects this room to the first one." muttered Billy.

"Hey. There's another room off to the right down here. It looks like it goes about fifty feet up to the right." said Toby.

IT'S THE BASS PLAYER!

"Just watch your step though. The ceiling's kinda low right here at the entrance." he warned.

They crawled up into this chamber of fallen rocks.

"I don't like the looks of this one." Corey said nervously.

"It looks like it could cave in at anytime. Let's get out of here." Toby answered.

They came back into the chamber with the water-filled hole.

There's a breeze coming from the left wall up about twenty five feet toward the hole to the upper room." said Donald.

As they climbed up the incline, Billy put his hand up to brace himself on a low hanging ledge of the ceiling. He felt something warm and fuzzy wriggle under his fingers. He jerked his hand back and lost his footing, causing him to fall on his backside on the floor. "You okay Billy?" asked Toby.

"Holey Crap!" exclaimed Billy as he pulled himself up. "There's something alive on that ledge there. I felt it!"

Toby shined his flashlight on the side of the ledge to reveal three little brown bats hanging upside down. Two were asleep, but the third one had been awakened by Billy's hand. The bat hung there, staring at them dully.

"Have we still got that peanut butter jar?" asked Toby.

"Yeah. It's still got a smidgen of peanut butter in it. Why? Are you hungry?" asked Billy. "Nah. We're gonna catch us a bat with it." answered Toby.

"Do what?" asked Corey.

"Yeah. We'll just take the lid off and put it over our little friend here, like this, and slide it to the edge of the ledge. Now give me the lid. Okay. I slide it off the edge, clamp the lid on like this, and there it is. A perfect specimen captured." stated Toby.

"Far out man! We've got ourselves a real live bat. Punch some holes in the lid so he won't suffocate Billy."

"Right Corey. Hey. You can take him to school with ya' and show him off in Biology class this fall. What are ya' gonna feed him though?" Billy said to Corey.

"Looks like he already found something to eat. If I didn't know better, I'd say he likes peanut butter." smiled Donald.

"We'll put him in the backpack. But I'll keep an eye on him every now and then, to make sure he's all right." answered Billy.

"Let's find out where that air is coming from." stated Corey.

They walked over to the north wall, where they found a small opening that was two feet by four feet. "The cool air is coming from here." said Corey. "We'll have to crawl on our bellies to get through there."

Billy scampered up through the small hole, leaving his back pack at the entrance. "There's a larger room up here!" he called back. "Come on."

Corey, Toby, and Donald quickly followed.

As they entered the tall, narrow passageway into the larger room, Toby shivered, "The temperature must have dropped twenty degrees in here. Look. This wall is dirt, instead of rock. I'll bet if we dug far enough, we'd come out on the side of the hill."

"Yeah. And you'd probably get buried alive doin' it too." replied Donald. "Come on. The cave goes this way. Hey Billy, wait up!"

Billy had climbed over a rise and down on the other side.

"There's daylight down here! Hey. We came out at the small cave entrance. Man! It's so cold down here you can see your breath." called Billy.

"Now we've got to turn around and go back through." stated Toby.

"What for?" asked Billy.

IT'S THE BASS PLAYER!

"Because we left the backpack with the bat in it. Remember doh doh?" answered Toby with a mock seriousness.

"Oh yeah. And I brought the fireworks too." added Billy.

They climbed back through the narrow tunnel that had never seen daylight, crawled back through the small hole where Billy left the backpack. They climbed back into the first chamber, and back out through the large cave entrance.

"Going down was a lot easier than coming back out." grumbled Corey as he crawled over the edge of the entrance back out into daylight once more.

"Look out! Cherry bomb time!" yelled Billy.

He lit the fuse on a cherry bomb firecracker, and hurled it into the main room of the cave. Rather than a loud echoing bang that was expected, there was only a muffled thud. "You sure those cherry bombs are good?" asked Corey.

"Yeah man. It's the caves that are a dud." answered Billy."I was expecting a big bang, and then a bunch of echoes. Well. Come on. Let's go." said Billy disgustedly.

"How's Barney the bat?" asked Toby as he watched Corey take out the peanut butter jar. "One thing's for sure. He likes peanut butter." answered Corey.

He put the jar back in the backpack and they headed down the hill.

They climbed back over the barbed wire fence at the bottom of the hill. As soon as Billy had climbed over the fence, he started jogging down toward the creek.

"Where ya goin'?" called Toby.

"Down to the creek to throw some m-80's in!" hollered Billy over his shoulder.

He had gotten halfway to the creek, when he slowed to a halt, while kicking his foot out to the side.

"EEEWWWW! Green cow patties!" he yelled.

"Let me guess. You just got fertilized!" snickered Corey.

"You got that right!" answered Billy. "Watch me get rid of that pile."

He pulled out one of his fireworks and placed it in the freshly laid manure pile. He lit the fuse and turned to run. As he turned, he tripped over a branch on the ground, and stumbled to catch his balance. By this time, the fuse had burned all the way down, and the M-80 exploded. Green fertilized shrapnel filled the air for about fifteen feet in every direction, including Billy's. As the smoke cleared, there was a dark green and brown polka dotted Billy standing there.

"OH crap!" yelled Billy.

Toby, Corey, and Donald took one look and fell on the ground rolling with laughter. "That's the magic word all right." laughed Toby.

"Better go down to the creek and wash that mess off, or your dad will kill you." warned Corey, as he held his side laughing.

"Oh fuunneee. Haha. You guys wouldn't be laughing if it'd been you." said Billy trying to look serious.

"Oh come on Billy. Let's go down to the creek. Just be sure to walk down-wind from us." snickered Donald.

"Thanks." snarled Billy good naturedly.

They walked down to the shallow part of the creek where the cows waded across. Billy waded in knee deep and washed the green and brown, fly-drawing goo off of his clothes and head. The water was clear and clean, so he didn't smell like dead fish when he was finished. They started back across the pasture toward the gate and Fairmont Estates, where Billy, Toby, and Donald lived. The gate was another good mile and a half walk back. By the time they reached the gate, Billy was bone dry. The four of them split up and went their separate ways to their homes. Corey kept the bat.

CHAPTER 5

The Trip To Columbus

Fred's house was a bustle of activity that Friday afternoon. There was a constant stream of musical instruments and equipment moving from Fred's mother's living room, where the band practiced, to the rental trailer in Fred's driveway. Corey was in the trailer packing the amplifiers, drums, P.A. equipment, etc. Toby, Paul, and Ben were in the moving stream of packing up, and moving the equipment out to the trailer. Fred was on the phone, getting final directions on how to get to the Officer's Club at Columbus Air Force Base. Corey always made sure the heaviest equipment was up front in the trailer, so it wouldn't fishtail at higher speeds when they were traveling. The P.A. speakers, Leslie 900 keyboard amplifier, and large guitar amp speaker cabinets went in the nose and front of the trailer. The organ, drums, cord cases, microphones, guitars, stands, etc. went in the middle and the back. Donna had not gotten there yet while the trailer was being loaded. It wasn't expected of her to load or unload the trailer, since, as Fred put it, she was only expected to sing and look good. Ben had borrowed his Dad's nineteen sixty eight Pontiac Bonneville, because it had enough power to pull the trailer and a carload of people easily, which is exactly what it had to do. The last piece of equipment was crammed into the back of the very full trailer. Then the doors were shut and locked. "Whew! I'm glad we don't have anymore equipment, or we'd have to rent a bigger trailer." expounded Corey.

"Tell me about it. Hey Miss Baddin's here. All that's left to load up now is us." said Toby. "Yeah. Lesh get loaded, then we'll get in the car. Hic!" teased Corey in a fake drunken voice.

"Nine thousand comedians out of a job and he tries to be funny." Paul said sarcastically as he rolled his eyes.

"You boys look like you've been having fun." greeted Donna as she walked up.

"Well, well. What planet did you come from? I see your antennas are showing. Ha ha." chuckled Ben.

"What's the matter? Doesn't your wife ever wear rollers in her hair?" retorted Donna. "Yeah. But not out in public." answered Ben.

"Well. There's nobody HERE that I'm trying to impress." stated Donna flatly.

"OOOh. what a cut." smiled Corey.

"I think she was referring to all of us boys." chimed Paul.

"Well Donna. We still love you too." said Corey with a twinkle in his eye.

"Where's Fred?" asked Donna.

"He's on the phone, I think." answered Toby.

Just then Mrs' Litton, Fred's mother, came to the door.

"You boys about through with that trailer?" she asked.

"Yes ma'am." they replied.

"Oh. Hey Donna. I didn't see you standin' there. Y'all come on in here and wash up. I got a mess of fried chicken y'all can eat before you leave out. I know you boys ain't gonna eat a square meal between now and Sunday mornin'. Donna, you come in here an' eat somethin' too. You look like you don't eat enough to keep a bird alive, bless yore heart."

Everyone acquiesced as Mrs. Litton made her way back to the kitchen.

IT'S THE BASS PLAYER!

"That's what I like about Mrs. Litton. She's got our best interests at heart." smiled Corey. "The only interest you're concerned about is your stomach." quipped Paul mischievously.

The six of them sat down at Mrs. Litton's table and indulged in some of her delicious southern cooking. She had prepared plenty of fried chicken, mashed potatoes, gravy, black eyed peas, cornbread, and fresh corn on the cob. And for desert, some banana pudding. After finishing, they all thanked her abundantly for the great food, or,

"The palatable delights for which we have partaken." as Corey said in his best W.C. Fields voice.

They all got in Ben's dad's car and headed for Mississippi. Ben was driving, Donna rode in the middle in the front seat, and Fred on the passenger's side. In back were Corey, Paul, and Toby.

As they were about five miles down the road, Corey looked up and said, "Hey Ben. Aren't you going the wrong way to Mississippi?"

"Don't worry. I know a shortcut. Besides, we're headed in a westerly direction anyway. Just relax and enjoy the ride." answered Ben.

Twelve miles later they topped a hill on a two lane black top to see the road end at a river, but there was no bridge spanning the waterway.

"Looks like your shortcut isn't so short after all." called Corey from the backseat.

"Take a look over on the other side of the river, gentlemen, and tell me what you see." answered Ben.

"A little flat boat." said Toby.

"Look again." prodded Ben.

"It's a ferry!" exclaimed Corey.

"What? You mean some homo is drivin' that boat?" asked Paul.

"No. Noodle head. He means an auto-ferry. You know? One that takes people and cars across rivers and stuff." answered Toby.

"Well. I ain't ridin' with no homo on no boat." said Paul, trying to sound convincing. Everybody looked at Paul and said, "Right! Okay!" while they rolled their eyes.

Ben pulled the car down to the edge of the water, where the ramp would set when the ferry pulled up to the east side of the river. When the ferry had stopped on their side and let down the ramp, Ben pulled the car and trailer onto the flatbed boat and parked it. Everyone got out to enjoy the ride. Corey and Toby had walked up front away from everyone else.

"You think Fred will ever get over Donna?" asked Corey.

"Who knows? There's something about your first love that you never get over." answered Toby.

"Sounds like you're speaking from experience, Tobe." observed Corey.

"Yeah. Something like that." sighed Toby.

Corey decided not to pursue the subject matter any further.

He started singing, "Riding on the ferry across the Coosa River. The boat's a rockin'. Makes my liver quiver."

"Hey. That's kinda catchy. You ought to write a song around that." interjected Paul as he walked up.

"That's what I'm doin'." smiled Corey.

Toby walked back to the car and leaned on it. He thought about all the good things he was enjoying, and yet, there was still a hole in his life that couldn't be filled at this point. He thought that maybe the void would go away when he was dating his last girlfriend, but it was still there. He couldn't figure out exactly what it was, but something was missing. When her mom decided to send her to an all girl college to keep her

IT'S THE BASS PLAYER!

away from Toby, because her mom didn't think Toby was good enough for her daughter, Toby decided to end the relationship. He simply did not believe in long distance relationships. He had carried on a penpal relationship with a girl in Savannah for several years, and only saw the girl once every two years. The last time he went to see his penpal, he had come in the front door and the girl was sending her local boyfriend out the backdoor. So he knew long distance love letter stuff just didn't work for him.

Corey walked up.

"Hey. Did ya' notice somethin' about last Saturday night Tobe?" he asked.

"No. What?" countered Toby.

"Did ya' notice that nothin' weird happened until after we played "The Pusher" by Steppenwolf right before the third break?" continued Corey.

"Yeah. Come to think of it, everything seemed okay until after we did that song. Of course, it being a full moon that night and the fact that the American Legion Post never had a black couple come in their club before might have had a little to do with it." replied Toby.

Corey looked up and said, "I guess you're right. I guess I'm making something out of nothing."

"Maybe. Who knows? Maybe God doesn't want us to do that song." Paul suggested. "After all, it is using God's name in vain in the chorus. Who knows?"

"Duh shadow do boss." chuckled Corey.

The three of them smiled at Corey's attempted humor. Nothing more was said as they stood there enjoying the scenery as they rode across the Coosa River on the old ferry. They had no way of knowing, or really caring that in five years, the old ferry, which had seen service for several decades, would cease to be. All traffic crossing the Coosa River would have to cross in Childersburg, twelve miles north of this spot. A piece of local history that would one day be forgotten. And no bridge would ever be built to span this part of the Coosa River.

At approximately seven p.m., the Pontiac, with it's cargo of musicians and equipment, pulled up into the front parking lot in front of the Columbus Air Force Base Officers' Club. Fred got out and told everyone to stay put until he could find out where to unload the equipment. He came back out after about ten minutes and instructed Ben where to pull the car and trailer to a side door next to the dining area and dance floor. Once again the stream of equipment and instruments started moving onto the stage to be assembled. By eight fifteen everything was set up and tuned. Then the motley road crew, which had set up the equipment and instruments, disappeared into their cocoons, better known as bathrooms, to transform into flashy, nicely dressed entertainers. After Fred had gotten dressed, he went to the bar to get a beer. The advantage of being his size was that he had no trouble buying alcoholic drinks. Who would question a guy who looked like a pale version of the Incredible Hulk about his age? Toby could have had the same advantage if he'd desired. He wasn't six feet three inches and didn't look like a football player, but he was stocky built and had enough facial hair to pass for a man well over twenty easily. He didn't care about this so-called advantage that all of his old high school co-horts would give anything for, though. He was content with drinking his seven up. He went to the bar to join Fred.

"Hey Tobe, This is Olga. She's our Swedish bartender for the night." said Fred.

"Yah. Aye feex der goot drinks for de cute moosicians. Vat veel yooh have?" Olga asked Toby.

"Oh yah. Aye haven der spriten in der glasen. Das ist goot. Yah?" Toby answered in his mock Swedish.

IT'S THE BASS PLAYER!

"Nutting but der sprite? Vas ist wrong vees dees kid? Aye tell yooh vat. Aye feexin der Olga special, und ist on Olga." she said.

"Vas ist dat?" smiled Toby.

"Der Singapore sling. Only very leetle weeskey in der drinky so yooh don' get drunky." She said as she winked at Fred.

"Okey dokey then." agreed Toby.

The blonde bartender went to the back to fix the drink. Fred turned to Toby and said, "Hey Tobe. What a ya think of Miss Creamjeans?"

"I thought her name was Olga?" countered Toby.

"Yeah. She may be Olga to you but she's Miss Creamjeans to me. Think I'll try to put her in my pocket and take her home." wist Fred.

"I don't think she'll agree to that." joined in Corey, who had just walked up. "Besides, you're not her type, Fred. I am. I mean, look at it from her point of view. She looks like the type that would go for the intellectual type guy, like me. Not some muscle bound jock." kidded Corey.

"Actually, I'm just enjoying the VIEW from where I'm at." Fred said as he watched her backside as she shook up the drinks.

"Man. It's getting deep in here." grumbled Toby good naturedly.

"Und whoo ees thees?" asked Olga as she walked back over with the drinks and gave Corey the once over glance.

Corey beamed back. He reached over the bar, took her hand, and said, "Hello gorgeous. My name is Corey Gable. You know? Like Clark Gable? I am overjoyed at making the aquiantance of such a lovely lady."

Corey leaned over and kissed her hand.

"Aah. A gentleman een der crowd. Do yooh play vees dees band?" smiled Olga.

"As a matter of fact, my dear, I am the main ingredient that keeps this band together on stage." Corey was laying it on thick.

Fred could only sit there, roll his eyes, and mumble, "Oh brother."

Toby chimed in, "That means he's our drummer. And an excellent one at that."

Corey turned and smiled. "Well thanks Tobe."

"Yooh are very charming Mr. Gable. For dat I feex yooh der Olga special too." she said. Corey asked, "Oh great. What is it?"

Toby piped up, "It's a Singapore sling. Man! These things are great."

"Uh Tobe. I'd slow down on that drink. We don't want a bombed bass player tonight." said Corey.

"Relax. She said there's hardly any whiskey in it. You can't even taste it." Toby maintained.

"That's the kind of drink you have to watch out for. They'll sneak up on ya' when you least expect it." stated Fred.

Toby said, "Okay. I'll slow down. Hey! What the?"

Everyone turned to see Paul and Donna come walking up with their arms around each other.

Corey greeted them with, "Hey dreamboat."

Paul spoke up, "We appreciate all the kind words."

Corey retorted, "Not you shipwreck."

Paul gave a sour look and said, "Ah. You're just jealous cause you don't have a gorgeous doll like Donna to make your entrance with and…Hey. Who is that?"

"Oh. This is my date when we get through playing tonight. Paul. I'd like you to meet Olga." smiled Corey as he winked at Olga.

IT'S THE BASS PLAYER!

Olga saw what was going on and went with the flow.

She said, "Yah. I am Mr. Gable's date tonight. He ees fine gentleman. Und whoo ees der young man vees der bleachy blonde?"

Toby thought, "This is where it hits the fan and we all get splattered."

"Uh oh. I think this is where we go tune up again." said Fred.

Toby thought, "Yeah. And it looks like these two gals are tuning up for a cat fight." Donna was looking daggers through Olga. "I'll have some hair-of-the-dog behind the bar." she said acidly.

"Vun bitches brew coming up." grinned Olga.

"Well now that we've established who we are, shall we dance to the juke box?" said Paul, trying to relieve some of the tension.

The juke box was playing the Tennessee Waltz.

"By all means. Let's." answered Corey as he grabbed Paul and started an exaggerated waltz, dragging a confused Paul across the dance floor.

Paul pushed Corey away and growled, "I was talking to Donna."

Corey grinned back, "Well. She was kinda busy, so I tagged you, partner. Actually, you waltz pretty good, for a guy."

Paul saw through Corey's teasing and what he was doing and started laughing. Everyone at the bar had cracked up at Corey's antics, including Donna.

She said, "Corey. You are the biggest clown. You always know how to make me smile."

Fred turned to Olga and said, "Seriously, You ought to go out with me after we get through playing tonight."

"Sorry. But aye have date vees der Major." said Olga apologetically. "But aye geeve yooh phune noomber und address if yooh vant."

"I want. I want." said Fred.

Fifteen minutes later, the musicians had made their way to the stage and started the first set. Ben introduced the band.

"Good evening ladies and gentlemen. We're the Common Faith. I'm Ben Regis, your host, and we'll be serving up some top forty hits for the next four hours. I'd like to introduce the band to you. On lead guitar we have Mr. Fred Litton. On bass is Mr. Toby Martin. On drums and percussion, Mr. Corey Gable. On keys is Mr. Paul Thornton. And our fair haired beauty, the Common Faith's heart-throb, Miss Donna Baddin."

Paul was supplied with a pitcher of draft beer from Olga. So was Fred. She made sure everyone had plenty to drink. Singing has a tendency to dry out your throat, so it's always good to have something to wet your whistle. Olga knew this, so she kept them supplied with water and whatever else they were drinking. The music was played to perfection up until the third set. The band performed together so well, that it seemed like they were all part of one musical instrument. The vocals were excellent. The dance floor was packed on every song. They sang and played songs by Three Dog Night, the Grass Roots, the Rolling Stones, Dionne Warwick, Karen Carpenter, James Taylor, the Beatles, and even threw in some old country classics like Your Cheating Heart by Hank Williams. In the second set they played a soul serenade medley back to back of the old songs, Hold On

I'm Comin' by Sam And Dave, Knock On Wood, Mr. Pitiful, She's A Lady by Tom Jones, and My Girl by the Temptations. They ended the soul serenade with Chain of Fools by Aretha Franklin, featuring Donna on vocals. As each forty five minute set ended for a fifteen minute break, the requests to keep playing would fill the air. Donna was approached by many

IT'S THE BASS PLAYER!

officers, but she didn't show any real interest until Olga's Major came and asked her to dance. She didn't stop with just one dance. It was during the third set and she was supposed to be on stage to finish out the last three songs. The band had just played "Easy To Be Hard" by Three Dog Night. Ben went into a comedy routine with the audience about football teams while Fred quickly took off his guitar and hot-footed it across the dance floor to Donna. "Please excuse Miss Baddin, sir. But she has to finish this set with us. I'm sure she'll be happy to come back out here when she gets through with the next couple of songs." apologized Fred, as he pulled Donna back to the bandstand.

"You've got some nerve!" hissed Donna.

"You can scream at me later. First let's finish the show. Think of the money." Fred said with a grin.

As Fred and Donna got back on stage, Ben was finishing a football joke that had the audience hysterical.

"Yeah. They wear orange on Saturdays to the game, and on Sundays to help direct traffic into the church parking lot, and the rest of the week on their job picking up trash on the side of the road."

As soon as the laughter died down, Ben introduced Donna one more time.

"And now we'd like to introduce the heart of the Common Faith, Miss Donna Baddin. She's going to sing a couple of tunes for ya, while I take a pause for the cause, if ya know what I mean." Ben said in his best Groucho Marx voice.

Donna sang a song by Karen Carpenter, then one by Dionne Warwick, and finally one by Carole King. The band finished the set and got off the stage for a break. All except Paul. He was having trouble getting up from behind his keyboard, after drinking all that draft beer Olga had sent him. Toby and

Corey helped him up and escorted him to the couch in the men's room.

"Tell Mizz Creamjeans she makes duh best beer in dis place. Hic!" slurred Paul.

"We've got to sober him up before the next set. Here Corey. You take these wet washcloths and put on his face, and I'll get Olga to fix some coffee for him." said Toby. "You guys is great! Y'all take such good care of me. Where's Donna? I gotta tell her I want her body. She's in love wif me you know. Hic! I'm horny!" said a drunken Paul. "Shut up Paul. We've got to get you sober before the next set, if that's possible." fussed Corey.

Corey bathed Paul's face with a cold wet cloth.

"Oh! I'm gonna be sick!" Paul got up, staggered over to the toilet, and emptied the contents of his stomach.

"How's Paul?" Fred asked Toby at the bar.

"Pretty well snockered. I thought he said he could hold his liquor." mused Toby.

"He can. He just can't deal with draft beer." smiled Fred.

"Olga's made him some coffee. Maybe that will bring him around." said Toby, as he headed back to the men's room with the coffee.

As he came in, he saw Corey sitting on the couch.

"Where's Paul? I brought him some coffee." asked Toby.

"He's looking for Huey, that drives a Buick, and goes to Europe every year, with Ralph." Corey grunted in a retching manner, pointing at one of the stalls.

"Hey Paul. Are you drowning in there? Just hurry up and get sober enough so you can go back and play soon." Toby said with urgency in his voice.

Paul moaned, "Ooh. You guys may have to…urk! Start without me."

"Well. I guess we can go back and do the songs we did without a keyboard that we did at the American Legion. After

IT'S THE BASS PLAYER!

all. We've been pretty much playing without a keyboard man for the last month and a half." grumbled Toby.

Corey piped up, "Sure. Why not? Paul. if you feel up to it, you can join us anytime during the last set."

"Thanks guys. I owe you one." Paul managed between grunts.

Toby and Corey joined Fred back at the stage.

"Where's Ben and Donna?" asked Toby.

"Ben's gone to call for reservations at the Ramada. Donna is out there in the blue yonder with major catastrophe." answered Fred.

Corey asked, "Who? "

"You know. Miss Creamjeans' boyfriend." Man! Olga's hotter than four wood burning stoves about this. I'm gonna have a talk with Donna when we get through. If anything happens to her, her dad will break me into little pieces." groused Fred. "Where's Paul?" he asked.

Corey said, "Oh. He's hugging the porcelain god looking for Ralph. I guess we can always do the tunes we were doing at the old cut-em-up, shoot-em-up joint last weekend."

Fred grumbled, "What is this? Mutiny? First Donna takes off with Major mistake, and now Paul's too drunk to play from all the beer!"

"Aye cap'n. It's mutiny olroit. But me and Mr. Christian eer will man the foresail and batten down the atches an we'll moyk it through the storm. You'll see." Corey growled in his best pirate's voice.

"Shiver me timbers. Aye. That we will laddy!" agreed Toby.

"Aye. That's because we're the three Muskyteers. Hey. Here comes Dartanyan."Fred was pointing at Ben as he was walking towards them.

"Ooh. Fred cut a funny! Actually though, he looks more like Porthos." snickered Corey, referring to Ben's slight beer belly.

A puzzled Ben asked, "What?"

"Never mind Ben. Looks like it's the four of us for the last set. Paul's too drunk and Donna is off in the wild blue yonder." explained Fred.

"I get the picture. I'd hate to be in Donna's shoes if Olga ever gets hold of her." grimaced Ben.

"Well. Let's finish this sucker. Break down, pack up, and go to the motel, so we can have our well deserved nervous breakdown." said Fred.

About halfway through the last set, Paul rejoined the band on stage. He was still three sheets in the wind, but he didn't miss a note or get sick anymore. Donna never came back to the stage for that last set. The Common Faith finished the last song of the last set, thanked the audience, who yelled for more, and left the stage.

Ben noted that, "It's always been a good sign of good showmanship to leave them yelling for more."

After the crowd had cleared out of the dance hall area, the road crew, consisting of Corey, Toby, Paul, and Ben, started breaking down the equipment. Fred went out trying to locate Donna. By the time the equipment was loaded back in the trailer, Fred showed up minus one female vocalist.

"Donna's gonna ride to the motel with the Air Force guy. Whataya say we get a couple of six packs to go and head on over to the motel." he said.

Paul piped up, "I'm all for that man. After I threw up, I felt good as new again. Too bad we can't take some of that draft beer with us."

Toby mumbled, "I can't believe this guy."

CHAPTER 6

Meanwhile Back at the Motel

After getting a couple of six packs from Olga and apologizing for Donna's actions, the five of them got in the car and drove to the motel. They pulled up into the motel parking lot and locked the car and trailer up. Fred went to get the keys to the two rooms. The five guys had two full size beds to share in their room, while Donna had a room of the same size to herself. The guys knew that one of them would most likely be sleeping on the floor in their room, since they were all too much of a gentleman to sleep in the extra bed in Donna's room. Fred took the guys up to their room, after he left word at the desk for Donna with the key to her room. After he let the guys into their room, he went to get a coke out of the vending machine down the sidewalk. He stood at the machine for a while, drinking his coke and thinking about things. Finally, Fred came back to the room to find a wrestling match going on between Corey, Toby, and Paul. Fred decided to join in. Corey, Toby, and Paul were all wrestling and tumbling on the floor.

Ben said, "Look Fred. It's Tojo Yamamoto, Len Rossi, and Sol Weingerhoff. Famous wrestlers from the Birmingham auditorium."

Ben saw the look on Fred's face and said, "Uh oh wrestling fans, It looks like Andre the Giant is about to step into the ring."

Fred growled, "Waaah!" and dove into the tangled mass of bodies.

Paul and Corey rolled back out of the way when he dove. Needless to say, he landed flat on top of Toby. Fred sat up on his knees to take on Toby. But Toby didn't move. Toby laid there motionless on the floor.

Paul stepped closer. "My God! His face is white as a sheet. Is he dead?"

Fred patted Toby on the cheeks and pleaded, "Come on Tobe. Snap out of it. Will ya? Come on. This ain't funny."

Corey said, "He'll be alright. He's just having one of his black out spells."

"Black out spells?" asked Fred.

"Yeah. Don't you remember? He said he blacks out occasionally because he has what they call atypical seizures caused by epilepsy." answered Corey.

Paul turned and said, "I thought most people who had it went into convulsions. You know. Fits, when they had epilepsy."

Corey answered "Nope. There's different kinds of epilepsy. The kind he has isn't that bad."

Just then, Toby's eyes fluttered open. He grinned and yelled, "Yaya heeheehee!", as he shook his hand at the end of an extended arm, gesturing like a chimpanzee.

"You scared the crap out of us Tobe." Fred breathed with relief.

"Aw. I was faking it just to see what you guys would do." said Toby.

It was obvious he didn't convince anyone in the room, including himself.

Paul jumped up and said, "Hey. Wanna watch Donna turn four shades of red?"

"What are you gonna do Paul?" asked Toby suspiciously.

IT'S THE BASS PLAYER!

"Watch this." grinned Paul.

"Famous last words of a redneck." mumbled Corey.

Paul wasn't listening. He stripped down to his BVDs, went over and knocked on the door adjoining Donna's room to the boys' room.

A voice inside said, "Come in."

Paul pushed the door open, went running into Donna's room, and jumped up and down on the bed opposite the one that Donna was laying in reading a book.

Paul jumped up and down on the bed yelling, "I'm horny! I'm horny!"

Donna never looked up from her book she was reading. She never made one single movement which would suggest shock or even surprise.

She called without looking up, "Fred. Would you come get this little kid out of my room?"

Paul stopped hopping up and down on the bed, turned beet red in the face, and ran back into the other room. Fred came into Donna's room.

"I'd say Paul has had one too many tonight." smiled Donna.

Fred answered, "Yeah. I'd say so too. He doesn't handle drinking beer too well. He's got a bunch of problems at home too."

Donna simply looked up and said, "Oh. I see."

She didn't, but she saw no reason to pursue the matter further.

"If anybody else knocks on your door tonight, ask who it is and then DON'T let em in." advised Fred.

"Thanks Fred. I won't. Goodnight." she said.

Fred turned and closed the door behind him.

"Dagdrattit! I wish I wasn't such a gentleman at times." he muttered to himself.

Corey looked up and said, "Say what Fred?"

"Nothin'. Think I'll take a soak in the tub." Fred spoke slowly. "You guys try to behave while I'm in there."

"Yes daddy!" Corey and Toby said simultaneously.

Paul would have answered too, but he was busy chug-a-lugging another beer. He gave a thumbs up. Fred went in the bathroom to run his water for a tub bath. He had just settled in the tub, beginning to unwind and about to doze off when, all of a sudden, the light went off.

"Okay. Who's playing with the light?" he growled.

Corey was at the light switch on the wall outside the bathroom door, snickering, "Watch this."

He started flipping the switch back and forth very fast, causing almost a strobe effect in the bathroom. Fred was struggling to get out of the tub, slipping and falling several times as he stumbled out onto the floor.

"Cut it out! I'm gonna break somebody's freakin' neck!" he yelled.

Just then Corey flipped off the light, ran, and dove onto the second bed. Everyone was laughing at Corey's antics when the bathroom door jerked open, and a large, muscle bound arm and hand came around the corner of the wall, and slammed against the light switch, followed by a loud "Waaah!" from Fred.

"Uh. Fred. I think you missed." guffawed Toby.

"Atta boy Fred!" laughed Ben.

Corey was laughing so hard he fell off the bed. Everyone, including Fred, laughed until they were laughed out. Except for Paul, who had passed out earlier. Then they all got ready for bed and crashed for the night. They drew straws over who would sleep on the floor. Paul got that priviledge since he was already out though. Corey put a pillow under his head and a blanket on him.

IT'S THE BASS PLAYER!

He said, "Well. At least he can't throw up on the bed now."
They knew morning would come too early, so they all laid down for the night. . It was now after three a.m.

At seven thirty the next morning Ben and Donna went down to the motel pool to sit and enjoy the quietness of the early morning hours.
"I'm starved. How about you?" Ben asked Donna.
"Yeah. I could use some breakfast. Let's go over to the restaurant next door." answered Donna.
"Okay. But we need to get the rest of the boys up first." replied Ben.
He looked up on the second floor where their rooms were and saw the motel maid one door down from theirs.
He called up to her, "Hey ma'am. Tell those boys in room two twelve to get up!" "What?" she called back.
"Just stick your head in the door in two twelve and tell those boys to get up!" Ben called back.
The maid nodded in understanding. She walked to the door, unlocked it with her key, poked her head in, and stopped. The sight she beheld in that room made a tornado aftermath look like Mr. Clean's kitchen.
She cleared her throat and said, "Uh. Y'all's daddy said for y'all to git up."
She quickly closed the door and pushed her cart on down the walk, muttering profanities and expletives under her breath. Inside the room, one pair of eyes popped open when she had peaked in. After the door had closed, Toby laid there chuckling to himself.
He mused, "I wonder who daddy is?" He got up and counted heads. "Yup. Just as I thought. Ben."
He poked his head out the door and called down, "Whata ya want man? It's not time to check out."

"I suggest if you want some breakfast, that you get a move on!" Ben called back."Breakfast?" blurted Corey as he came out of a deep sleep. "That's the magic word." Corey and Toby quickly got dressed, poking at Fred's and Paul's feet to get them up. Then they went downstairs to join the others for breakfast. They were halfway through their eggs, grits, ham, and toast when Fred and Paul finally showed up. From the look on Paul's face, Fred had said something to him about his conduct the night before.

"Fred. I'd like to talk to you when you get through eating." said Donna.

Fred looked puzzled and said, "What about?"

"I'll wait till you get through. Then we'll discuss it." she answered.

Fred wondered what was on her mind, dismissed it, and ordered his food. Soon only Fred and Donna were left at the table. The rest of the band had gone back up to the motel room to get ready to leave. Though they were very curious about Fred and Donna's conversation, no one mentioned it. They packed their belongings back in Ben's trunk and waited for Fred and Donna. One half hour later, Fred showed up.

"Guess you guys have already figured out what's goin' on. Huh?" he said slowly.

"Let me guess. Donna's quitting. Right?" surmised Paul. "Look. If it'll make any difference, I'll go apologize and beg her to stay. Man! I acted so STUPID last night!" Fred put his hand on Paul's shoulder.

"No need to do that Paul. It's not you. She just doesn't want to do the traveling gig thing. She just thought we were gonna play around the Chalaka area. She's given her notice. Said she'd do the gig tonight and next weekend at Craig Air Force Base in Selma. But that's it."

IT'S THE BASS PLAYER!

Corey looked up and said, "Now who was it that reminded somebody else about the picture jinx?"

Toby turned and mumbled despondedly, "Oh give it a rest. Will ya Corey?"

"Okay. But maybe someday you guys will listen." retorted Corey.

Ben spoke up, "Let's load up. We gotta take the equipment over to the Servicemen's Club and set up."

Paul said, "Yeah. We can't sit around here crying over split blonde hairs. Speaking of which. Is she riding with us or what?"

"Nah. she's riding there with Major you-know-who." answered Fred.

Ben turned and said, "It figures."

CHAPTER 7

The Base Tour and the Service Club

The guys loaded up in Ben's car and drove back onto the Air Force Base, stopping at the gate to get directions to the Servicemen's Club. They parked on the backside of the club and started the human train that carried the equipment into the dance hall area. After setting up the equipment, they decided to run a sound check, by going over a couple of songs. When they finished the second song, Fred suggested that they practice on a few new songs. he practice session drew several servicemen, who were sitting behind them. After working on an old Jimi Hendrix tune, Fred heard a room full of voices behind him. He turned to find that, sure enough, there was almost a whole room full of servicemen, who started calling for more. So the practice session turned into a jam session. Many songs later, Fred looked at his watch and noticed it was two thirty in the afternoon.

He said, "Let's go grab a bite to eat. I'm starved!"

Corey answered, "Sounds great! Hey. You guys will have to come back tonight when we crank up."

One corporal spoke up, "Hey. Where's the chick that's supposed to be in your band? There's one on the poster out front."

"You mean we have a poster with our picture on it?" asked Corey excitedly.

IT'S THE BASS PLAYER!

"Yeah. So where's the chick?" persisted the corporal.

"She's out sightseeing on base, I guess. Hey. Is there any place we can get some thing to eat?" he asked.

"Sure. There's a canteen down at the end of the hall and to your right. Take a left and you'll run into our pizza and beer pub. And civilians are always welcome. Especially dudes who can play like you guys." volunteered the corporal."My name's Mike. This is Jeff and Ken. The guy at the end of the table is Masher. Show em why they call you masher."

Masher grabbed up an empty beer can and flattened it against his forehead.

"Far out!" exclaimed Corey.

"This is Fred, Ben, Paul, Corey, and I'm Toby. The ah, chick's name is Donna."

The corporal asked, "Where are you guys from?"

"We're from a little town in Alabama called Chalaka." answered Toby.

Corey chimed in, "Better known as Buzzard's Roost to all the local yokels."

Mike wrinkled his nose, "Buzzard's Roost?"

Toby alleviated, "Yeah. It's an old Creek Indian name or something. But so much for our town's history. Where are you guys from?"

Mike answered, "I'm from Black Oak, Arkansas. The rest of these guys are from all over the place. Come on. I'll treat you guys, or y'all as they say down here, to some beer and pizza."

Paul spoke up, "Man. I'll oblige you on the pizza, but you can keep the beer."

After they finished several pizzas, Mike said, "Hey. would you guys like a tour of the base?"

Corey belched after eating three fourths of two large pizzas, and said, "Yeah man. That would be cool!"

Mike turned and said, "Okay. My car's outside. We can all ride 'cause it's a station wagon with three rows of seats."

They piled into Mikes's car and left the parking lot. As they drove around the base, Mike speeled off facts and points of interest about the base in a monotone comparable to a typical tour guide.

As they rode by a tall fence topped with razor wire, Toby exclaimed, "Hey man. Those are B-52's! There's one, two, three,…I count about ten or twelve out there."

As he pointed to the large jets sitting off across the asphalt behind the fence.

"They've got armed guards and guard dogs around those babies." noticed Toby.

Mike answered, "Yeah. And there's a red line painted on the ground around where each of those jets are parked. That's to let everyone know that if anybody sets foot across those lines without proper clearance, they will be shot on sight. No questions asked." Paul let out a low whistle and remarked, "Wow. Talk about security being tight. It's tighter than Toby's last girlfriend's chastity belt."

Everyone rebuked Paul in unison, "Can it Paul!"

Paul scoffed sarcastically, "Well excuse the heck out of me."

"Wonder if they've seen any action in Nam?" asked Fred.

"Yup. They just flew back in from a bomb run over Hanoi two days ago. They can leave with full ordinance, refuel in midair. Drop their load, and skeedaddle back here, all within a twenty four hour frame." answered Mike.

The tour moved on around the base, and finally ended up back at the Servicemen's club. The band and their new friends went inside to the T.V. room, relaxed, and swapped small talk. Some of them dozed while passing the time. Paul was snoring fairly loud in the recliner he was in. At seven thirty, the band

IT'S THE BASS PLAYER!

assembled in the large restroom to change into their playing clothes. Fred was the last one to come in.

Corey looked up and said, "What's the long face about Fred?"

Toby moaned, "Don't tell me. Let me guess. Our fickle female has flown the coop." Fred replied, "You hit the nail on the head, Tobe."

Toby said, "Say no more."

"Yeah. Her football jock boyfriend showed up and talked her into going home with him, instead of doing this gig. Naturally she said yes." explained Fred.

"I know some servicemen who are going to be pissed when they don't get to see blondie when we play." groaned Paul.

Ben snarled, "Thanks for the uplifting thoughts."

Corey asked, "What are we gonna do Fred?"

"What else? Tell everybody she got deathly ill and had to go home. Then do our show without her anyway." answered Fred.

Toby went and found their new friend Mike, and explained about Donna. He asked Mike to explain to the other servicemen from the stage about Donna. Mike got on one of the microphones and told the audience about Donna.

Several of the guys in the audience hollered, "Who needs her? Bring on the Common Faith."

The Common Faith pulled off an excellent show, to which the response from the servicemen was a chant of "Damned Good Band!" after every set. In the third set, Fred started the first four bars of a song that was too familiar to everyone on stage and in the audience. A sudden shudder of dread came over Corey. Toby caught the same vibes.

He went over to Corey and said in a low voice, "Tell me we're not doing "The Pusher" by Steppenwolf."

Corey just nodded. "Looks like we're in for it now." he grimaced.

The band proceeded to play this song, which, in the chorus, it condemns drug pushers. The one problem Corey and Toby had with the song was that it used God's name in vain in the chorus. Ben refused to sing it for that reason, so Fred sang it. Toby made a mental note to discuss dropping the song from the play list after this gig. The night went on without mishap, as they played the rest of the third set and their fourth. When they finished, the servicemen kept yelling for more. At that time the entire band thanked all the servicemen for coming and that they would be back soon. The band left the stage and went to change into their roady clothes, and started the strenuous task of loading their band equipment back into the trailer for their trip home. Mike, Ken, Jeff, and Masher helped them tote the heavy stuff out to the trailer. And, as usual, Fred tended to the financial end of the bookings. Nobody really minded that Fred wasn't there to help load up the equipment. He had proved his knack for wheeling and dealing, when it came to getting a little more out of a gig than anyone else in the group could.

CHAPTER 8

The Long, Long, Long Trip Home

After the last piece of equipment was loaded into the trailer, Corey went to fetch Fred. Ten minutes later, Corey and Fred came back grinning from ear to ear.

"What's going on?" asked Toby.

"We just got booked back here in four weeks." beamed Corey.

"For a hundred fifty more and without the blonde bombshell." added Fred with an ear to ear smile.

Ben grinned, "So let's go home."

Fred said, "That's what I like about you Ben. Straight to the point."

They got in and pulled out of the parking lot. The car had traveled a full city block, when Ben pulled over.

"What's wrong Ben?" Toby asked from the backseat.

"Gentlemen. We've got a flat." Ben said ominously.

"No! Not possible! It can't be happening. We're in for it now."expounded Corey.

Paul droned, "Don't start with the jinx junk again."

Corey retorted,"But I've warned y'all and you just don't listen."

"Never mind that. Let's get that tire changed. Tobe, man the chains so we can take the trailer off and get the jack under the car." said Fred.

"Okay. Would you like to lend your manual dexterity to the situation, Corey?" asked Toby.

"Duh, Yeah man. Like I can lend one hand or two, or even a crab claw if ya get into a pinch, man." drawled Corey.

Paul chuckled, "Corey the crab strikes again."

Everyone pitched in to get the tire changed and the spare put on. The tire that had gone flat was on the rear on the passenger's side.

"Let's hope nothing else happens." said Fred as they finished putting the trailer back on the hitch after changing the tires.

Toby reset the chains. Corey turned to Toby with an "I told you so" expression on his face and started to say something.

Toby blurted, "I don't wanna hear it Corey."

Corey sighed, "Okay."

They got back in the car and started for home again.

Toby thought, "Well. At least the worst is over."

He settled back in the seat and closed his eyes to doze off. He was almost to the edge of unconciousness, when he was jolted back to being fully awake. He first noticed that the car wasn't moving.

"Are we stopped for gas?" he yawned.

"I wish that's all there was to it, Tobe." Ben replied.

"No. It can't be. Not again! Corey. I know what you're gonna say, so don't say it!" stammered Toby.

"I didn't say nothin.'"said Corey sleepily.

Fred asked, "Tobe. You wanna man the chains again?"

"Do I have a choice?" groused Toby. "Which tire is it this time?"

Ben answered, "The spare we put on. We at least got to downtown Columbus before it blew. There's a service station about three blocks back down that way. I can see the sign. Let's hope they're open late."

IT'S THE BASS PLAYER!

They took the trailer off once again and took the tire off the hub. Fred proceeded to roll the tire down the sidewalk, with Ben right on his heels. Corey found a concrete block and put it under the axle hub, just in case the jack slipped.

Then Toby, Corey, and Paul sat down on the curb to wait for Ben and Fred to get back, when a voice from behind them said,"What are you boys doin'?"

They all turned to see a bright flashlight in their eyes. They could make out a man in uniform, complete with badge and gun in holster, standing behind the bright light.

"We had a flat tire officer. And we're waiting for our buddies to get back with the tire fixed." volunteered Corey.

"Flat tire huh? What's in the trailer, boys?" the policeman drawled.

"Just band equipment sir." replied Toby.

"Band equipment huh. What kind of music do y'all play?" inquired the officer.

"We play the best durned country you ever heard this side of the Mason Dixon line, sir." Corey came back.

"Hey. That's all right. Y'all do any Hank Williams? asked the policeman.

"Is there any kind of music without a little Hank in it? smiled Corey.

"Shoot. I reckon there ain't." the officer smiled back. "Where y'all been pickin' at?" he asked.

"Somewhere back up the road at a local V.F.W. I never did notice which one it was though." lied Corey.

Toby thought, "I wish he wouldn't say shoot. Boy. Corey's laying it on thick. Keep talkin' Corey, and maybe he won't run us in for loitering."

"What kind of instruments do y'all play? asked the officer.

"Well. Toby there plays the bass fiddle. Paul there plays the pinnaner. I play drums. And our mandoleen picker and fiddle player are down yonder at the service station."

61

The policeman asked, "What's the name of y'all's band, so's the next time y'all are at the V.F.W. I kin come hear y'all."

Corey smiled as he laid it on thicker, "Maybe you heard of us. The Bugstompers? We usually play over in the Birmingham area."

At this point, it was getting harder and harder for Paul and Toby to keep a straight face. "No. Can't says I have. Well. You boys be careful goin' home now. I gotta finish patrolin' the block here. If y'all are back over this way again, give me a holler down at the station here. Just ask for Jim-Bob." the officer offered.

"Thanks. We'll do that. You be careful too." called Corey.

"Goodnight y'all." called the officer as he walked to the next block.

The boys called back, "Goodnight."

After the officer was out of earshot, Toby guffawed, "Bugstompers? Where'd you ever come up with that one, Corey?"

Corey snickered, "I don't know. It just popped in my head. That's what it looked like those old geezers were doin' at the American Legion back home. They called it dancin', but I call 'em the way I see 'em. Paul, you can get up now."

Paul was rolling from side to side, laughing and holding his stomach.

Fred and Ben walked up one hour later. The patched tire was put back on, and the trailer on the hitch. Naturally, Toby fixed the chains in place. Then they got back in the car to head for home again. This time Corey and Toby stayed awake for half an hour, waiting to see if there would be another blow out. At last, Toby decided it was safe to nod off to sleep again. He was sleeping soundly this time when Corey poked him in the side.

IT'S THE BASS PLAYER!

"Hey Tobe. Rise and shine and show your behind."

Toby muttered, "Are we at a service station? Man. I gotta go."

Fred spoke up, "Yeah. We're at a service station alright. Come on Tobe. Man the chains." Toby pleaded, "NO! Don't tell me. I know it can't be happening again!"

Corey answered "I'm afraid so Tobe."

Toby asked, "Which tire is it this time?"

"The same one we had fixed." replied Ben.

"And how far did we get this time? Four miles?" Toby asked sarcastically. "No. We actually made it to Tuscaloosa." answered Fred, as they disconnected the trailer again. Ben spoke up, "This time I'll get the tire in the trunk fixed."

Fred turned to Ben and asked, "Why don't we just use mom's credit card and buy a new tire? Y'all can pay me back later on it."

Ben answered, "No. We'll just get this other tire fixed and go home. I'm counting on some of that money we made to put back for the baby."

Fred resigned, "Okay. If you insist. But I think we'd be better off buying a new tire." "Well. You know what they say, third time's the charm. Maybe we'll make it home this time, Fred." said Corey.

"Maybe." was Fred's only reply.

Fred and Ben started rolling the tire from the trunk over to the garage they were parked next to. his time Toby crawled back in the car to catch a few more minutes of sleep. The sun was coming up now and it was hard to sleep. So he got back up, because he knew that once the sun was up, it would be too hot to sleep in a car that wasn't moving. He heard Paul cackling and giggling. He knew the "gone-too-long-without-sleep" sillies bug had kicked in. The strange thing about this disorder is, how contagious it can be. He got out and walked around behind the trailer. The sight he beheld was typical Corey humor. Corey had put his glasses on upside down, rolled up one pants leg up to his knee, and was doing a dance similar to a Mexican hat dance, singing "I've got syphillus, I've got V.D. I got it from my girl. Who could ask for anything more?"

Paul was holding his stomach, laughing so hard that tears were rolling down his cheeks. "Corey stop! I can't take anymore." Paul would gasp between hee haws.

Toby suddenly succumbed to the dreaded bug that had already taken hold of Corey and Paul.

"Hey you! I'm from outa town! Don't hang around if I got diarrhea!" Toby growled as he hunched over, curled one arm under his chest, and dragged one foot as he hobbled over to Corey.

"Oh no. It's a Cleep! Corey exclaimed in mock terror.

"A cleep. What's a cleep?" snickered Paul.

"It's sort of like a drunk talking werewolf with horns." answered Corey.

"What kind of booze does he drink?" laughed Paul.

"What else? Green Cleep whiskey that he makes in his still down in his Cleephole." growled Toby.

Then Corey went back to singing, "I got snifflus, I got gone rear. I got a Cleephole. Who could ask for anything more?"

They all burst out laughing uncontrollably. Toby started his Red Skelton routine of holding his elbow up and letting his forearm swing limp back and forth. Staring at it, he swatted his wrist, causing his arm to swing in a complete arc and hit himself on top of the head, upon which he acted like he was dazed. Forty five minutes later Fred and Ben came around the trailer with the patched tire.

"Do you guys ever get serious?" smiled Ben.

IT'S THE BASS PLAYER!

"We have to laugh to keep from crying in this situation." answered Paul.

"Good point." added Fred.

They changed the tires out one more time, and put the trailer back on the car hitch. Got back in, and headed for home again.

Fred said, "I wish you would've let me get a new tire Ben. I don't feel comfortable with that may pop on there."

Ben said, "Look. If it'll make you feel any better, Fred, if we have another blowout, you can buy a new tire with your mom's card. But I don't foresee another one. So let's not worry about it. Okay?"

Fred caved in, "Okay. If you say so."

The car had driven about twenty miles and just passed the city limits sign for Centerville, when the back of the car felt like the whole underside was dragging on the pavement. Ben slowed the car and pulled off the road on a long straight stretch of this two lane blacktop.

Fred simply turned to Ben and said, "Well?"

"Okay. You win my friend. Let's go buy a tire." was all Ben could say.

Once again everyone did their duties to remove the tire. This time the tire had been chewed to pieces when Ben pulled off the road. Luckily the rim was in good shape. Fred and Ben had started to walk up the road toting the tire because it was too badly chewed up to roll it, when a tow truck went by going in the opposite direction. The truck turned around, came back, and pulled up beside Fred and Ben.

An older, grisly looking character leaned across the seat and said, "You fellers look like you could use some help."

"We sure could." piped up Fred.

"Well. Come on. I'll give y'all a lift to town." the old man volunteered.

Fred threw the tire in the back of the tow truck, as he and Ben climbed in the cab. The truck pulled off and drove out of sight.

"This is getting completely ridiculous. And all because we played that one song." grumbled Corey.

"It could have been worse. We could've played that song twice last night." Toby came back.

"Good point. No telling where we'd be if we'd played it twice." agreed Corey.

Nothing further was said until Ben and Fred returned with a new tire an hour later. Fred and Ben thanked the old geezer for the ride back and forth from the service station.

"Anytime. You fellers be careful now." was the old fella's only reply as he waved and pulled off.

This time the tire was put on with hew hope and enthusiasm instilled in everyone. The band got back on the road once again. This time they made it back to Fred's house without a single mishap. It was twelve noon on Sunday. Everyone was exhausted, but they managed to unload the trailer. It took three hours to drive to Columbus and twelve hours for the return trip home. Toby hoped that this night would never repeat itself again. Everyone got into their cars and they all went home, tired and worn out.

CHAPTER 9

Playing at Selma.
Donna's Last Performance

The following Saturday the band was once again loading up to go play.

"You're sure Donna is going with us on this trip?" Toby asked Fred.

"Yeah. She said she and her boyfriend are going to follow us to Selma. So when she gets through, she can take off with him." answered Fred.

Corey came out of the back of the trailer looking like someone had poured a bucket of water on him.

"You're not hot, are ya' Corey?" smiled Ben.

"Nah. Not at all. I just look like somebody turned a firehose on me." Corey said sarcastically with a twinkle in his eye.

Fred would be pulling the trailer with his Pontiac GTO. Fred, Corey, Paul, and Toby would be riding in Fred's car while Ben would ride with his brother, Pete, in his nineteen seventy Ford Maverick. Donna and her boyfriend, Larry, would follow Pete's car in Larry's car. Pete had asked the guys if he could sing some backup with his big brother, and the guys had said that was fine. Pete didn't want any pay, he just wanted to sing with the band. They left Fred's house and headed to Selma, Alabama, to Craig Air Force Base there. They were booked to play at the

Officers' Club for that night, thanks to Markus Attractions. They drove down highway twenty one to Montgomery, then turned onto highway eighty west, which took them straight to Selma and Craig Air Force Base. "Hey guys. Whata ya think about making a demo tape in a recording studio?" asked Fred over his shoulder, while they were headed down to Selma.

"Oh man! That'd be cooler than cucumbers." answered Toby.

Everyone else chimed in, "Yeah man. Cool!"

Fred said, "You know. It wouldn't cost that much to do a demo tape at Prestige studios in Birmingham. That's where Donna, me and the old Common Fate cut that forty five that Lindy Martin payed for."

"You mean you, Donna, D.R., Clyde, Tim, and Gary Bird? The first band?" asked Corey.

"Yup. That's where we cut it." answered Fred.

"I'm kinda glad you didn't want to use the exact same name with us that you used with them." asserted Corey.

"Yeah. They were all good musicians and great guys, but they ain't us." added Paul. "Yeah. Using a similar name though was a good idea." said Toby.

"Who named the other guys Common Fate Fred?" asked Corey.

"One of my neighbors, Mike Holt. He came up with two names actually. Chosen Few and Common Fate. Everybody voted for Common Fate." answered Fred.

"Well. WE are the Common Faith and WE are perfeshonals." stated Paul.

"Okey dokey then." said Toby with a twinkle in his eye.

They arrived at Craig Air Force Base at six o'clock that evening. They pulled up to the gate at the base. Fred got

IT'S THE BASS PLAYER!

directions from the guard at the gate, to the Officers' Club. Fred also told the guard that Pete's and Larry's cars were with the band too. The guard motioned Fred's, Pete's, and Larry's cars on through.

As Pete and Ben rode through the gate, Ben said, "Hmmm. Maybe I should think about enlisting. I'd definitely be able to take care of Lanett and the baby, and have a career to boot."

Pete turned and said, "You've got to be kidding me. With all this crap about Vietnam? I'm shocked you would even think about it."

"Well. It was just a thought, little brother." answered Ben.

"You can't do that. Those guys are counting on you. This is the best band you've ever played with. Maybe dad can come through on getting you on at Kimberly Clarke with him." Pete said as he pointed to the car in front of them.

"Well. Like I said, it was just a thought." repeated Ben.

They pulled up at the Officer's Club and got ready to unload while Fred went in and inquired where the stage was. He came back out and gave directions where to take the equipment.

"Corey. You're in charge of getting everything set up on stage. I'll unload the trailer. The rest of you guys can haul it in to Corey."

"Wait a minute, Fred. I always load and unload the trailer. What's up?" asked Corey.

"I just thought I'd give you a break, Corey. You're always sweatin' to death in the trailer." smiled Fred.

"Well. Uh, thanks Fred." beamed Corey.

Fred unloaded the equipment. Toby, Paul, Ben, Pete, and Larry, Donna's boyfriend, hauled it inside to the stage. Larry picked up one of the P.A. speakers by himself, which normally would take two of the guys in the band to move.

"Hey. Don't you want some help with that?" asked Toby.

"Nah. I lift heavy stuff like this out on the football field all the time. They're usually carryin' a football though." answered Larry.

"Okay. But don't rupture yourself." cautioned Toby.

Larry smiled, "No problem."

Larry hauled the speaker cabinet in to the stage.

Toby muttered, "Better your back than mine."

After the equipment was unloaded and hauled inside, Fred locked up the trailer and parked the car and trailer in two parking spaces in the parking lot. Even Donna was helping set up the band equipment. She helped run cords to the P.A. system and hook up microphones. She helped get a vocal sound check on the microphones. Everyone did their part to get ready to play.

Toby came over to Fred, who was on the other side of the stage from Donna, and said in a low voice, "I'm kinda glad Larry's here. Maybe she'll stay on stage tonight for the whole show."

Fred turned and frowned and in a low voice said, "Well. It may be okay for you he's here, but not for me."

"What? Oh. You're not comfortable with him and Donna together. Is that it?" asked Toby.

"Something like that." answered Fred.

"Well cheer up Fred. Who knows? Maybe you'll run into another Olga here. I know that'd make you feel better." suggested Toby.

Fred smiled, "Yeah I just wish Olga didn't live so far away. If she was here that'd brighten my day for sure."

Corey walked over and said, "Did I hear someone mention Olga? Man she sure made my heart go pitty pat. Don't fret my friends. We'll be going back over there in three weeks. And I'm sure Fred will be ready and able for a date with that heavenly creature."

Fred smiled, "Yeah. Think I'll give her a call a week before we go over there, and see if she'll go out with me the weekend we're there."

"Now that's the old Fred we all know and tease." grinned Corey.

The band finished setting up. They all went to get a bite to eat at the restaurant, since the man in charge of the restaurant said it was on the house, since they were the entertainment that night.

After they ate, they went and changed into their "playing clothes". The band started playing at eight o'clock. They played two sets of forty five minutes each, with a fifteen minute break in between. They did their usual variety of top forty tunes. There were many requests for more country tunes, so, as one of the officers put it, they could "rub bellies" more with their dates. After the second set, they went on break, at which time some of the officers got on the microphones to auction off some things for a worthy cause.

When the bidding for the items got slow, one of the guys on the microphone would holler "Okay you weenies! Show ya hair!"

That's all this guy would say on the mic, but it was so loud, that it hurt Corey's and Toby's ears. After the auction was over, which lasted about thirty minutes, the band came up and played a long set until twelve, which was the latest they were allowed to play on a Saturday night at the club. Donna was on stage all night with the band. Ben asked her to sing a few more songs than she normally sang. She was happy to oblige. The band played the last song and said goodnight to calls from a full dance floor of "More!"

At the end of the last set, Donna turned to the band and said, "Hey y'all. I don't know how to break this to you, but, well, this is my last night with y'all. This traveling thing is just not for me. I've enjoyed singing with you fellas, and Corey is always making me laugh. And Paul, you're a mess! But I can't do this anymore."

Ben and Fred looked at each other and shrugged their shoulders, with a look of "I knew this was coming."

Ben said, "Well. Okay. We enjoyed it while you were with us. We'd be lying if we said we won't miss your face."

They all came over and hugged Donna's neck except Fred. He just shook her hand and said, "Good luck."

Fred then went over to Larry, who was sitting at a corner table, and had an inaudible conversation with him while the rest of the band started breaking down the equipment to load back into the trailer. They loaded it all back into the trailer. This time Fred packed the trailer while Ben went and got their pay for the night. Everyone got in their vehicles after Ben came out and they left.

"By the way, Fred. How much did this gig pay tonight?" asked Corey.

"Six hundred dollars. Ben will pay everybody when we get back to my house." answered Fred.

"You mean we made a hundred dollars a piece? Man! That's the most money we've made yet for one night!" Expounded Corey.

"Yeah. Markus Attractions has found us a gold mine." smiled Fred.

Nothing else was mentioned about Donna quitting, since they all half-way expected it. They all knew too that Fred still had feelings for her, so they didn't want to "pour salt into an open wound" by discussing it. They drove back to Fred's house, unloaded, got their pay from Ben, and went home.

CHAPTER 10

The Good News, the Bad News, and the Ugly Theft

"Wait a minute! You're telling me that we are actually going into a recording studio Saturday?" Toby asked as the rush came over him again.

"Yup" answered Fred.

"Tell me all of this again, so I make sure I heard right." babbled Toby.

"Okay. I've called Kenny Wallace at Prestige recording studios in Homewood, to set up a recording session for us to do a couple of tunes from our show, and a couple that you and I have written. After we get the demo tapes, I am to hand one copy over to Mrs. Beige, Paula Spiegel's mother, to give to the Cowsills' manager, for an audition for us to be the opening act on tour."

"Isn't that the studio where your last band cut that forty five a couple of years ago?" asked Toby.

"Yeah. That's the one." answered Fred as he wrinkled his nose.

"Oh yeah. I remember you said Donna messed up the words to the song on one of the vocal tracks, and had to redo it a couple of times." smiled Toby.

"Yeah. She couldn't read my writing too well. The first time through she sang "Who's that strange lump starin' in my window every night." Fred smiled back.

"Man! Wait till Corey hears about the studio. He'll flip out! It is definite that we are going. Right?"

"Yeah. Oh, and we've got a booking Saturday night at the Club apartments in Homewood, compliments of Mrs. Beige also." continued Fred. "We need to practice every chance we get this week to be ready. Especially on our own tunes. Ben hasn't gone over any of this original stuff with us yet, so he's got to learn how the vocals go."

Toby asked, "Which tunes of ours are we gonna do?"

"Well. I thought we'd do the Railroad Song, The Air Is Dead, and Daylight." answered Fred.

"Daylight. Isn't that the one about that sexy dream you had?" smiled Toby.

"That's the one." snickered Fred.

"I think we ought to do a couple of Three Dog Night tunes and maybe a couple of others." Added Toby.

"That's a good idea Tobe. That way we can show off our vocals a little bit. The only problem is, we're only going to be able to cut five or six songs at the most. But I guess we can figure out which cover tunes when we get there." answered Fred.

"Wow. Maybe this is our big break, Fred. And we owe it to Mrs. Beige." Toby chattered excitedly.

"Let's not get our hopes up yet, Toby. Nothing has happened yet, so let's wait till it does." cautioned Fred.

"Yeah. But this is the closest we've come to, quote-unquote, making it big." Toby gestured with two fingers of each hand like quotation marks in the air. "Hey. I think someone's knocking at your front door Fred. I'll get it."

Toby opened the front door to find a very disgruntled Ben standing there.

Toby called over his shoulder, "It's just old golden throat himself."

IT'S THE BASS PLAYER!

He turned back to Ben and said, "Man. Have we got some good news for yous today." Ben said, "Good. I could use some good news for a change, Tobe. Let me sit down and tell you what's goin' on with me first. You know my wife, Lanett, is pregnant, right." "Right. I mean it is a little obvious that she is, or else she's been eating watermelons whole without chewing." teased Fred.

"I'm serious Fred. Now listen. You also know how hard it's been for me to land a good paying job. In fact, if it weren't for us staying at mom and dad's house, and the income from the band, we'd be up the creek without the proverbial paddle."

"Yeah. So?" interjected Fred.

"Well. I've been offered an opportunity to have a steady job for the next twenty years, with a substantial income, and instant insurance to cover Lanett and the baby. My uncle has offered it to me."

"Hey. That's great Ben. Go for it!" blurted Toby.

"But you haven't heard who my uncle works for." warned Ben.

"It shouldn't matter if he works for the creature from the black lagoon. Take the job, Ben." stated Toby.

"My uncle is the local recruiter for the U.S. Army." groaned Ben.

"Oh crap! Don't take it Ben. That's not so great." moaned Toby.

"Wait a minute. It's Ben's life. He's got to do what's best for him and his family, Tobe. Have you decided if you're goin' in or not yet?" said Fred.

"Not yet. But I do need to let him know something before next week. Now what's the good news you fellers were wantin' to tell me?"

"Oh not much to tell, except we may have a shot at the big time. That's all."

"What's he talking about Fred?" asked Ben.

At that question, Fred proceeded to explain the recording session, the contacts with the Cowsills, and the booking Saturday night to Ben.

"Well. I would've never dreamed! Boys. Maybe there's hope for us in this band after all. I think I'll hold off on enlisting just yet." grinned Ben.

"Please do for now. Oh yeah, we've got another booking Friday night in Columbiana. Markus Attractions is on it's toes bringin' in the dough." remarked Fred.

"Well. As to the Cowsill thing, I don't care so much about the fame as I do the fortune right now." smiled Ben.

"Are we ready?" asked Fred, as he sat down in the driver's seat in his GTO.

"All aboard and ready to boogy!" called an excited Corey from the back seat.

"Yeah man. Let's do it." agreed Toby.

"Okay. We're on our way." acknowledged Fred.

They backed out of his driveway, pulling the U-haul trailer once more. As they pulled out, Ben and his younger brother, Pete, followed in Pete's Ford Maverick once more. They all drove to Prestige Recording Studio in Homewood, Al, babbling excitedly all the way about making what they called, the big time.

"I think the choice we made on the songs to do is excellent, Fred." said Paul.

"I know one thing. We practiced on 'em enough this week that I was playing 'em in my sleep." groused Toby good naturedly.

An hour later they pulled into the parking lot in front of the studio.

IT'S THE BASS PLAYER!

"Well. Here we are guys." Fred called over his shoulder as they pulled around behind the building.

They all got out and went inside for the session. Fred went through the introductions of the band members to Kenny Wallace, the owner of the studio.

"Okay Fred. I've got most of the booths set up, except for the vocals. That shouldn't take but a few more minutes, and then we'll be ready. By the way, Toby, is it? Would you prefer to use your bass, or the Fender bass here in the studio?"

Toby quipped excitedly, "You mean I can use your bass here in the studio? Wow! That would be cool!"

"Well. I'm just gonna use my trusty old Gretsch Country Gentleman guitar, if you don't mind Kenny." volunteered Fred.

"Whatever's comfortable for you Fred." replied Kenny. "Ben. We'll have your vocal booth set up in a few minutes."

Toby immediately went over and tenderly picked up the Fender Precision Bass guitar, while the rest of the band got their instruments and vocal chords ready for recording. "What about our backup vocals, Fred?" asked Toby.

Kenny came over and asked, "You're gonna have backup vocals too? Okay. No problem. What we'll do is run down a dummy vocal first with the music. Then we'll come back and pull the dummy vocal off and put the main and backup vocals on at that time." Corey piped up, "Wait a minute. Who's he calling a dummy? Is he wanting me to sing?" "No Corey. What he means is, Ben will sing a vocal track along with the music, so we won't get lost in the music. Then Kenny will go back and replace the main vocals with better main vocals along with the backup vocals." explained Toby.

"Oh. Okay. I knew that." grinned Corey.

"Then why'd you...Oh never mind!" exhaled Fred, realizing that Corey was just making a joke.

They recorded the six songs without very many problems, except Fred's extra loud guitar, giving Kenny and especially Corey a headache. Each time Fred would hit one of his high notes on his guitar, Corey would almost come unglued, because his headphones in the drum booth had no volume controls. So he was catching the full force of Fred's licks in his ears. After the second take, Corey finally ripped off the headphones and threw them on the floor. Since he could see Toby directly across from him, and he could hear Fred on the phones on the floor, he had no more problems with the session. Part of Toby's and Corey's groove, as they called it, came partly from watching and listening to what each other was doing musically. This helped them think and perform as one.

When they finished the music tracks on the six songs, Corey came out of his booth squealing, "FRED! Can't you play at a lower volume? I mean, there are other numbers on your volume knob besides ten!"

Fred droned back, "Yeah. But with my amp, that's the only way to get enough distortion and sustain to hold notes."

"Well. Why don't you invest in a foot pedal distortion box, like everybody else?" asked Ben's brother, Pete.

Fred just rolled his eyes and said, "Gee guys. Think of the money."

"I'd rather think of saving my ears." chuckled Toby.

"Everybody's a comedian." sighed Fred.

Next came the vocal tracks. Ben's vocals went down as smooth as silk. Then came the backup vocals. Fred, Toby, and Pete got a good laugh when Kenny played back just the backup vocals without the music.

Toby said, "That sounds like the Lemon Sisters singing backup."

Corey said, "Don't you mean the Lennon Sisters?"

Toby smiled, "No. It sounds like some sisters that ate too many lemons."

Ben's brother, Pete, had added a fourth part on the backup harmony vocals with Fred and Toby.

Mrs. Beige, who looked like a young Debbie Reynolds, came in with her two beautiful blonde daughters, Brenda and Paula. Fred went over to greet them. Fred quickly introduced the rest of the band members to Mrs. Beige and her daughters. Kenny was getting ready to play the final mix on the songs, when Harold Spiegel, Paula's husband, came in frowning.

He groused, "Hey man. Who's the dumb S.O.B. that left the trailer full of band equipment open in the alley? I just chased off two punks who were checking it out."

"Oh my God! The equipment!" Toby exclaimed as he ran out the door.

Corey was right on his heels. The doors on the trailer were open. Toby crawled in, checking to make sure nothing was gone. He found everything but his bass guitar. His forty dollar Audition bass guitar from Woolworth's was gone.

He thought, "The cheapest instrument in the trailer, MY bass guitar, is gone."

Toby sat there in shock.

"I can't believe someone would take my bass guitar" he said exasperatedly.

"The only thing I can figure Tobe, is that they didn't have time to grab anything else but your bass." said Corey.

Anger boiled in Toby as he said, "If I ever catch the butthole who took it, I'm gonna beat the crap out of 'em! I'll kick his butt till his nose bleeds!"

Fred said, "Sorry Tobe. Let's lock up the trailer and finish the session. Tobe, we'll get you another bass."

"But that was MY bass!" exclaimed Toby.

They locked up the trailer and went back inside to finish the session. Harold volunteered to sit outside by the trailer and stand guard until they got through. Kenny made two master copies on seven and a half speed tape reels. He also mixed the songs down in stereo. Fred gave one copy to Mrs. Beige, and kept the other, in case they wanted to make some records from their original tunes.

Mrs. Beige asked Fred, "Are you boys still going to play at the clubhouse at my daughter, Brenda's apartment complex?"

"Yes ma'am. What time do we start playing?" asked Fred.

Mrs. Beige replied, "You can start around nine if you like. You boys can hang out at Brenda's until time to set up. I'll see if I can get hold of Mrs. Cowsill, and tell her I have your band's tape to send her. I may just take it to her myself."

All of the band thanked Kenny Wallace for the great recording session.

Corey, Paul, Ben, and Fred all went down to the pool to relax and hangout for the afternoon, after they arrived at Brenda's apartment complex. Toby was down in the dumps about his stolen bass. He sat on Brenda's couch after taking some aspirin for his headache.

He sat there for a while, when Mrs. Beige came in and said, "Toby. I have someone on the phone that wants to talk to you."

"Somebody wants to talk to me? Who?" he asked.

"Just somebody." replied Mrs. Beige.

He got up, wondering if it was his mom. He walked into the kitchen where the phone was, and picked up the receiver off the counter.

"Hello?" he said.

A young female voice said, "Hey. Is this Toby? The famous bass player for the Common Faith?"

IT'S THE BASS PLAYER!

He answered, "Yes. This is Toby Martin. Who is this?"

She answered, "This is Karen Cowsill. Mrs. Beige told me about your bass getting stolen while you guys were recording. I'm sorry to hear that. Mom says soon as Mrs. Beige can get us the tape, she'll sit down with our manager and listen to it. It'd be nice to have you guys go on tour with us. I can't wait to meet you guys."

"That'd really be cool." smiled Toby for the first time that afternoon. "How old are you Karen?"

Karen replied, "I'm ten. How old are you?"

"Nineteen." replied Toby.

"We're taking a break from being on the road 'cause my brother has the flu. They're talking about making a T.V. show about our family. They're going to call it the Partridge Family. I don't know why they want to name us after some birds or something." she said.

"Well a bird on T.V. is worth a Cowsill on the road any day." snickered Toby. "Well. I hope that works out for y'all." he replied.

"For who?" giggled Karen.

"For y'all. I mean yous guys, as they say in New Joysey." Toby teased.

Karen laughed, "I love to hear southern people talk. It's so different."

"Well shazam! Ah kaint wait till we'uns kin come up thar an make music together, y'all." drawled Toby. Karen was giggling very loudly.

"Weyull. Allratty then y'all. Hope to see you-uns real soon." she snickered.

"Well allratty thar little lady. Y'all take care then." he drawled back.

"Bye Toby. Tell all the guys I said hey." she said.

"I will." Toby hung up the phone.

He went over to Mrs. Beige and hugged her neck.

"Thanks for brightening my day." he said.

"It's the least I could do, since some dim-wit took your bass. But I've also got some good news about y'all playing tonight. Brenda has found you a bass guitar you can play tonight. One of her friends has one you can use." said Mrs. Beige.

Toby hugged her neck again. "Thank you, thank you, thank you. Can I adopt you as my second mom?" smiled Toby.

She grinned, "I would be honored Toby."

Brenda had just walked in from the pool. She was still wet from swimming in the pool. Toby went over and hugged Brenda's neck.

She looked slightly shocked and said, "What's that for?"

"For finding me a bass to play tonight." grinned Toby.

"Oh shoot. No problem hon. Glad I could help. You sure can't stand up there and hum the bass parts." she said smiling. "Of course, now you're going to need a towel to dry off, since I'm still soaked from swimming." Toby just smiled back, "Who cares. As long as I still get to play tonight, I'll play waterlogged if necessary."

Later that evening, the guys came in from the pool. Toby asked Fred and Corey if they would like to go with Brenda and him to borrow a bass guitar from Brenda's neighbor, Bob Barker.

Corey piped up, "You mean Bob Barker of Truth or Consequences?"

Toby smiled, "Yeah. Same name. Different guy."

They went over to Bob's apartment. When they had gone inside to talk to Bob, Toby noticed a Fender Stratocaster that was broken up pretty bad. Bob had all kinds of musical equipment, but Toby was drawn to the Strat.

IT'S THE BASS PLAYER!

"Man. Somebody didn't like your Strat too well." said Toby.

Bob turned and said, "Oh that. If you'll notice the autograph on the body, you'll know who and why it's busted."

Toby leaned over and read the name scrawled on the body of this broken guitar. His eyes grew wide as he realized it had been played and broken by his musical hero.

He stammered, "J,J...J, Jimi Hendrix?! Okay. Now you got to tell me the story on this baby."

Corey came rushing over to look at the strat.

"Not a whole lot to tell. I was working sound for the Tuscaloosa Coliseum when Hendrix was there. This was the only guitar he played that night. When he got through playing, instead of busting it up against the amplifiers or beating it on the floor, like he was known to do, he..."

Toby interrupted, "He took it off and threw it up in the air and let it hit the stage, causing a feedback that almost deafened everybody. I know. I was there. I was off to the right, about half way up in the stands. I can't believe you have THAT guitar! Can I touch it?" Bob smiled, "Sure. But not the autograph. I don't want it smeared. I've been thinking about putting it in a glass case, just like it is."

Toby touched the neck and body and said, "Man. This is a piece of history. That was my first rock concert, and you have the guitar Hendrix played."

Brenda said, "Well Tobe, looks like your day is getting brighter by the moment."

Toby turned to Bob and said, "I'm not gonna hug your neck like I did Brenda's, but I will shake the hand of the man who made this day the best one yet."

He shook Bob's hand. Bob handed Toby his Gibson EB-3 bass guitar and said, "Take good care of my baby, here. I'll be over to the clubhouse tonight to pick it up when you guys get through."

"Wow. First I played a Fender bass in the studio today, and now I'm going to play a Gibson bass tonight. The two biggest names in bass guitars." babbled Toby excitedly. Corey said, "Hey. Maybe I need to let somebody steal some of my drums. Maybe I might get to play on Buddy Rich's set."

"You mean Mr. "best drummer in the world"?" asked Toby. Corey smiled, "Yup. The same."

After they all got back from Bob's apartment, they went over to the clubhouse to

set up and play. The band started playing at nine o'clock. They played their usual forty five minute sets with fifteen minute breaks in between. On the fourth set, a guy came up to Fred between songs and requested Jeremiah was a Bullfrog.

Fred said, "Oh. You meant Joy To The World by Three Dog Night. Yeah. We can do that."

The guy said, "Great. I do appreciate it."

He stuck out his hand to shake Fred's hand. When Fred pulled his hand back after shaking the man's hand, he noticed the man had handed him some folded up pieces of paper. He looked down in his hand to discover the man had given him five hundred dollars. He looked up to see that the man had blended back in with the rest of the crowd on the dance floor.

In shock, all he could say was, "Well. I'll be a mud-beaten horny toad."

The band played Joy To The World and dedicated it to that "Guy" that wanted to hear it. When they finished playing at one o'clock, Fred came over and gave each one of the band members a hundred dollars each, along with what the club paid them for playing.

Toby and Corey took their extra hundred a piece and turned around and gave it to Ben and said, "This is for the baby."

IT'S THE BASS PLAYER!

Ben objected, but Corey and Toby wouldn't have it any other way. They packed up and went back over to Brenda's apartment. Toby gave the bass back to Bob Barker and told him how much he appreciated it.

Bob said, "No problem. Glad I could help. Who knows? I might need to borrow something from you sometime."

Toby decided this had been the best weekend yet, even with his bass guitar being stolen. Harold Spiegel volunteered to let Toby use his bass guitar until Toby was able to buy another. The guys decided to party at Brenda's for a while and bunk down on the living room floor that morning. It was well after 3 in the morning before they finally settled down to sleep. Late Sunday morning, everybody got up to the sweet smell of breakfast cooking. Mrs. Beige had fixed breakfast for everybody. They ate a hearty meal, then thanked her for all her kindness and help.

"You know I have a motive behind all this. Don't you.?"she smiled mischievously.

"Naw. Not you! What is it?" asked Corey.

"I want to be your road manager / den mother when you guys go on tour." she said with a mock seriousness.

"You can be our den mother-slash-road manager anytime!" beamed Corey.

The rest of the band agreed.

Fred hugged her neck and said, "We'll see you soon."

She said, You can count on it."

They got in their cars and headed home.

CHAPTER 11

A Change in Personnel

The following Thursday Toby came over to Fred's house. Fred had called and needed to talk to Toby. So Toby came over, wondering what was going on.

"Come in and have a seat." sighed Fred.

"What's up Fred?" asked Toby.

"Well he did it. Ben joined the Army yesterday. He left this morning for Montgomery to take his physical. You know, after he takes that, he's gone to boot camp." droned Fred.

"I thought he was gonna wait and see what happens with the Cowsill thing." said Toby.

"I talked to Mrs. Beige Tuesday. She said that one of the brothers had become deathly ill, so they're not going anywhere for a awhile. I told Ben Tuesday evening, and he said he couldn't wait around for that ship to come in, so he went and joined yesterday. The upside of his joining, is that his uncle said he could guarantee that Ben wouldn't be going to Vietnam." answered Fred.

"Now I guess we've got to find another lead vocalist." grumbled Toby.

"Well Pete said he would fill Ben's shoes for now. But that's not all. There's more news." warned Fred.

"Oh God! Now what?" asked Toby cautiously.

"Well. You remember I said I had a scholarship to play football at one of the colleges here in Alabama?" asked Fred.

IT'S THE BASS PLAYER!

"Yeah. So?" interjected Toby.

"Well. I just found out the college is Troy State in south Alabama. That means I'm not going to be playing the football games and be able to play with the band on weekends too. Even if we played one night on the weekend, I couldn't afford to drive back and forth to play. So that means that you'll have to be in charge, Tobe, during football season. After that, I can come back and play. But it looks like you'll have to play lead guitar until then. You can probably get Harold Spiegel to play bass until I get back." said Fred. "Man! Talk about dropping a bomb in somebody's lap!" expounded Toby.

"Come on Tobe. There's no one else I'd trust to take over while I'm gone. Besides, you can use my trusty old Gretcsh Country Gentleman." coaxed Fred.

"Well. I appreciate you offering the Gretsch, but I'd just as soon use my dependable Fender Mustang. Your strings sit too high off the neck for my little fingers. It's a lot easier for me to bend the strings on my Mustang." stated Toby.

Fred asked, "So you'll do it?"

Toby looked up and said, "Well of course. But only until you come back from football season. We ARE the three muskyteers, even if you aren't here for a little while. Now let's just hope Paul doesn't go into one of his weird moods and decide to quit. You know how flaky he can be at times."

Fred said, "Well. Just remember it's just for a little while. I was thinking. You could get a second guitar player to play with you."

Toby smiled, "Well. You know Pete can play rhythm guitar if I need a second guitar. Besides, another guitar player means splitting the money six ways again, like with Donna."

Fred mused, "Yeah. I guess you're right Tobe. Think of the money. That's my philosophy."

CABOT BARDEN

The following week Toby got the new guys together with the band for their first practice. It felt awkward going back on lead guitar after being on bass for almost a year, and having someone else on bass. But the music still sounded pretty good. Pete's voice had a higher range than Ben's did, but he was always on key. It was like going from a Tom Jones baritone to a Steve Perry tenor. Toby was amazed at how quickly a four hour show came together with the new guys. This was a blessing since they had another booking coming up the next weekend at the Servicemen's Club in Columbus. Markus Attractions was keeping the band supplied with bookings. The weekend came for them to play the Servicemen's Club. They drove to Columbus with no problems. One of Toby's best friends, Johnny Major, put all the equipment in his Ford Econoline van and drove over to Columbus with the band. The band set up and played their four hour show. Toby noticed Olga showed up with her Major. She came up and talked to Toby and Corey when her date had gone to the bathroom, wanting to know where Fred was. They told her he was off playing football at Troy State.

"Aye vas hoping to see Meester Fred tonight too. EEs he going to come back und play vis yooh boys?" she said.

"He'll be back with us when football season is over. We'll tell him you were here and asked about him." smiled Corey.

"Aye hope yooh boys vill be back heer soon so I can see heem again." she said. "Aye see yooh got reed of the bleachy blonde voman."

"Yeah. She quit that same weekend we were here last." said Toby."We're so glad you came tonight. I just wish Fred could have been here for this."

Olga said, "Vell. Tell Meester Fred to call me first chance he gets. Aye vould love to see heem again."

IT'S THE BASS PLAYER!

Olga and her date stayed for the whole show that night. Many of the servicemen couldn't take their eyes off Olga. The only problem on stage was Harold. He was drinking all the draft beer he could hold. He got up off stage several times to go empty his bladder. He even got up one time right in the middle of a song and walked off stage to go to relieve himself. The band kept playing without a bass player and finished the song anyway.

At one point when Harold went to the bathroom, Toby looked over at Paula, Harold's wife, and said, "I'm glad you're driving home and not him."

Paula just rolled her eyes and nodded. When they finished playing, they loaded up the equipment and headed back to Chalaka. Paula asked Toby to ride with her and Harold back. After they got onto the highway headed home, Harold started in on Toby about doing acid.

"Yeah man. Acid is the best, man. You gotta try it just once. It'll change your whole life man."

Toby kept telling Harold he didn't care anything about doing drugs. Harold kept on babbling about doing LSD until he finally passed out. Paula noticed he got quiet.

Looked over and said, "Thank God! I didn't think he'd ever shut up. I am so sorry Toby, He only gets like this when he's had too much beer."

"It's okay. I kinda figured it was the beer talking." he said.

Toby decided to throw up a mental red flag about this. Harold was an okay musician,

but he obviously had a chemical and alcohol dependency problem. So Toby made a decision that night to look for a new bass player. On Monday, Toby called Paul's friend, Charles Grimes, and asked him if he'd like to play bass with the band.

"It's only temporary until Fred comes back after football season." explained Toby. "Then I'll be goin' back on bass."

Charles said, "Yeah. Bigger'n hell! I know I'm not no where as good a bass player as you Tobe, but yeah. I'd love to play with you guys. Maybe when you go back on bass, I could be a singer."

"Now there's a thought. Me and Fred will talk about it. Sounds like a good idea to me." said Toby.

Charles said, "Cool. Let me know when we're gonna practice."

Toby replied, "I will. I'll holler at ya later man."

"Okay man." Charles said and hung up.

Toby then called Harold and told him he was fired.

"That's fine. Y'all don't do enough heavy metal for me anyway. I'd rather play with a REAL rock band anyhow." replied Harold.

Thursday evening Toby and the guys, minus Harold and plus Charles, got together for practice at Corey's house. Everything went smoothly. Charles blended in well. Toby's worries about drugs in the band were gone for now. His realistic look at booze and drugs was, if you get caught drunk, you might go to jail for the night. But if you got caught stoned, with drugs on you and in you, you were looking at one to ten years in prison at least. Neither one is good for you, but at least the penalty for being drunk was nowhere near as severe. He called Fred and told him what happened. Fred was relieved that Toby had handled things so well. Toby also told Fred that Olga had asked about him when they had played at the Air Base. Fred said he would call Olga that weekend, since he still had her phone number. The band played a couple of more weekends at some frat houses in Tuscaloosa and Auburn. After the second weekend gig, Pete announced he was leaving the band and moving to Rome Georgia to go to Georgia Tech. Toby asked Charles to step up and be the lead vocalist.

CHAPTER 12

More Personnel Changes and the Death of a Friend

The week after Pete left, Fred came back to play. They put Charles out front as lead singer. Toby went back on bass guitar, using Charles' violin bass guitar, because Toby hadn't been able to save up enough yet to buy a nice bass guitar. The following weekend the guys were booked for a party Friday night at ST. Bernard College in Cullman, Al. and a frat party at Delta Chi frat in Tuscaloosa. They went to play the Friday night booking, only to get a very unwelcome reception by the crowd.

The crowd kept yelling things like, "You guys need to play more heavy metal."

One guy came over in front of the stage and kept yelling at Toby, "Hey man! Let me up there! I'll show ya how to play some cool heavy metal sounds on that bass!"

Toby just shook his head and kept playing. Paul got perturbed after the first set and told the rest of the band that he wasn't going to play anymore after that night, if that's the way people are going to be when he played. Fred kept assuring Paul that this was a one time thing.

The guy who had wanted to play Toby's bass kept coming up and yelling, "It's the bass player! Why won't you let me play your instrument Mr. Bass player?!"

When the band was packing up to leave, after they got through playing, the same guy came outside and started yelling "It's the bass player!"

He yelled several expletives which riled Toby. Toby picked up a piece of hardware from Corey's drumset.

"Just one lick across his skull!" hissed Toby.

Corey and Paul grabbed Toby saying, "Don't do it Tobe. He's not worth it."

Corey said. "Yah Tobe. I don't need to clean some a-hole's blood off my cymbal stand." The heckler realized his heckling had gone too far.

"Hey man. Don't get pissed. I was just raggin' you. I didn't mean no harm, man. But I am a better bass player than you'll ever be." he said as he staggered away.

Toby said, "Yeah. You'd better walk away, you piece of crap! "Cause I'll reshape that messed up skull for ya!"

Paul took a deep breath and said, "I'm done. I've had enough. And Fred and nobody else ain't gonna talk me out of it."

The band went home. Fred and Toby sat up in the front seat of Fred's car on the drive home, discussing their options of getting another keyboard player by the next night, to play the gig in Tuscaloosa.

"Well. There's one thing I can do. I can try to teach some of the songs to my brother, Mark, tomorrow morning, and maybe he can fill in till we can find somebody else. Paul won't be picking up his keyboard for a while, since he doesn't have anywhere to store it." said Toby.

"Great Idea Tobe. Maybe Mark can get us through the songs that need a keyboard." said Fred optimistically.

The next morning Toby and Mark were over at Fred's house going over the show. Toby had taken an erasable marker

Mike, Charlie Gamble, Me

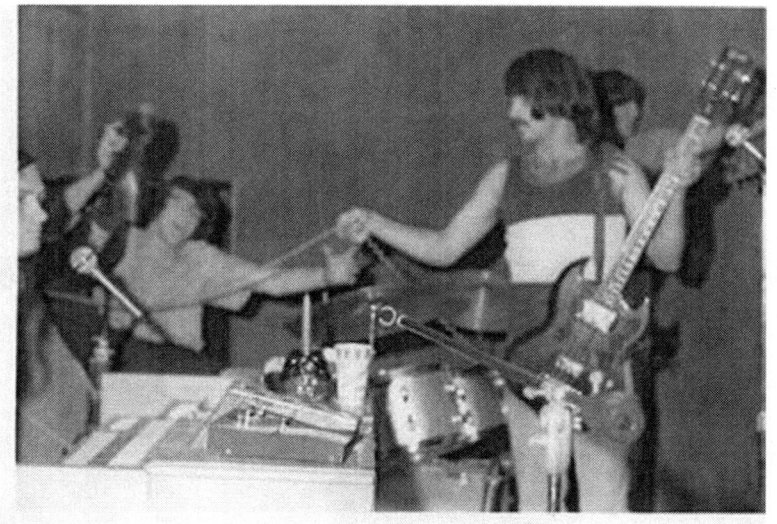

Ever tried playing smashed?

Hey, this isn't Abbey Road.

IT'S THE BASS PLAYER!

and marked the keys A,B,C,D, etc., so that Mark would know what key was which. He then wrote out the keys above the lyrics of every song, so Mark would know what chords to play on every song. They rigged up a small lamp to sit on top of the keyboard, so Mark would be able to see the book with all the chords in it, if it was dark in the room where they would be playing that night. In three hours, Mark had the entire show down. Mark always amazed Toby with his musical abilities. Before Corey had played drums with Toby and Fred, Mark was the original drummer for the band. But he and Fred just could not get along. Their personalities mixed like oil and water. But Mark was wanting to play again, even if it was with Fred, and playing keyboard. That night the band played at Delta Chi fraternity in Tuscaloosa.

By the third set the crowd was yelling, "Damned good band!" at the top of their lungs. Toby and Fred just looked at each other with a "How did this happen?" look on their faces. With Charles on vocals and Mark on keyboard, Toby was thinking that maybe there won't be anymore personnel changes again for a while.

Toby teased Fred when they were breaking down after they got through playing, "You better watch out Fred, because if Mark ever picks up a guitar, you can be replaced." Charles added, "Yeah. Bigger'n hell. Don't let him touch your guitar, Fred."

Fred said, "Oh hardeehar har. Funnneee! You guys are a barrel of laughs."

They finished packing up after the gig, feeling they had really done something good. They all agreed to never play ST. Bernard College again. They played at Union Springs the next weekend for some high school kids. The P.A. system blew a fuse that night. Fred started playing the Pusher and just before Charles could start singing, the P.A. system blew a fuse.

Corey looked disgusted at Fred, "I keep telling you we need to drop that song from our list."

Fred frowned, "I get the message Corey. Consider it dropped."

Luckily somebody actually had a fuse that fit in the P.A. amp, and the guys went back to playing and finished out the night. The P.A. fuse was the same as a car fuse, oddly enough. Nobody slept on the way home that night, for fear of a tire blowing out, like the first trip to Columbus and back. But they made it home okay without mishap. The next week, Paul came and picked up his keyboard. Toby happened to be at Fred's house when Paul came and picked it up.

He asked Fred after Paul left, "So what do we do for a keyboard for Mark. He sure can't play my dad's accordion."

Fred smiled, "Well. I may have some good news about another keyboard man. Birney Peters said he would play with us."

Birney was considered the best keyboard player in the Chalaka area. The only keyboard player that was better than Birney was his brother, Tommy, who had gotten married, and retired from playing in bands. Birney looked like your typical hippy, with long hair halfway down to his waist, an old tee shirt, multicolored striped pants, and corduroy house slippers, with no socks. The band practiced one practice with Birney and it was unanimous that Birney was in and Mark was out, except for Toby. Toby didn't like getting Mark's hopes up about playing with the band and then firing him shortly thereafter. It was a very uncomfortable situation for Toby. This was family. Since Toby's dad had died when he was eleven, he had always watched out for his little brother, to help keep him out of trouble. Toby and Mark had been close growing up. Toby's brother, Donald, didn't have much to do with Mark. Fred knew

IT'S THE BASS PLAYER!

this. So Fred told Toby if it would help, that he would call Mark with the bad news. Since he knew Toby didn't want to have to tell his brother.

One morning the next week, Toby was asleep, when his mother, Louise, came in from work and said soberly, "Tobe. Getup. I need to tell you something."

Toby mumbled, "What is it? Can't it wait till later?"

Louise said, "I'm afraid it can't Toby."

Toby's mother worked in the emergency room at the hospital on third shift, and had just come in from work. So Toby knew something bad had happened that night.

"They brought Charles Grimes in last night." she started, "He was in a real bad car wreck down towards Weogufka. They think he was driving too fast on his way home and lost control of the car. We don't know how long he laid there in the car before somebody found him."

Toby came fully awake and asked, "Is he okay?"

Louise started to cry. "Oh Toby. I'm so sorry. I'm afraid not. He was cut up pretty bad. I cleaned him up best I could and got most of the external bleeding stopped. But, I watched him die in my arms! He bled to death internally before we could do anything." she sobbed.

Toby and his mother sobbed on each other's shoulder. A couple of days later, Toby and the rest of the band went to Charles' funeral. It was a very sad day for the Common Faith. It was the only time Toby ever saw Birney wear a suit and tie. Toby thought about how fragile life really is, even though most young people his age always thought they were invincible, and did dumb things that were at the least, risky, if not dangerous.

When Toby came up to the casket, he muttered, "I hope God let's you in up there my friend. You deserve to be there now."

Charles' dad came over to Toby and said, "If you don't mind, you can use Charles' bass guitar for now, but we'd like it back soon, to have something to remember him by. I just wish we could have heard him sing with y'all. We heard him sing around the house, but we never got to hear him sing with a real band."

Toby said, "Thank you sir. He was a great friend and a really good singer. I know I will never forget him."

Mr. Grimes said, "Yeah. He always spoke highly of you boys. He really enjoyed singin' with y'all. Maybe he'll get to sing for his Lord now."

Toby held back the tears and said, "God bless you and your family sir."

CHAPTER 13

Don Frodo

The band waited a week to practice. Toby, Corey, and Fred didn't quite feel like playing for a little while, after the loss of their lead singer and good friend. Fred had lost his scholarship at Troy State and had to go to work in the local music store, Nelson Piano Company. Since he was working there, he got permission for the band to practice in the back room of the store after hours. Two weeks later, Toby decided to buy a Gibson EB-3 bass guitar from Fred's store. It was just like the one he had borrowed from Bob Barker, except it was brown instead of red. Fred had met a guy named Don Frodo, who claimed he could out sing anybody. Fred asked the guys about letting this guy sing at one of their band practices. Everybody said they didn't really care except Birney.

"You know Fred. We really don't need a guy who just stands out front and sings. Between Toby, you and me, we've got lead vocals and three part harmony. What more do you need? And we only have to split the money four ways, instead of five or six." stated Birney.

Corey said, "You know? He kind of has a point."

Fred spoke up, "Well I didn't promise this guy we were gonna hire him or anything. I just thought we'd see if he's as good as he says he is. And we've been five piece since Toby, Corey and I started this band."

Birney retorted, "Hey. Wasn't it you, Toby, his brother, and Ben Regis, when y'all started playing the eleventh frame a while back? That only counts as four."

"No need in arguing over technicalities, the point I think Fred is trying to make is, that we make enough for a fifth man when we play. Right Fred?"said Toby.

"Yeah. That's true. Even though my motto has always been "think of the money", We do make enough to pay a fifth man if we want to." answered Fred.

"Yeah. But do we NEED a guy who just stands out front and sings? I mean. I'm not giving up any of my songs I'm singing for some "Johnny-come-lately". Stated Birney. "Okay. Your point is taken. I'm just sayin' let him sit in and see if he's all that good or not." replied Fred.

"Okay by me." Birney caved in.

The next practice the following week, Fred brought Don in and introduced everybody. "Toby? That's an odd name. You don't hear it much these days. But then, I can't say much with the same last name as a hobbit, stuck on me." said Don.

"What?" asked Corey.

"You know? Like in the book, Lord Of The Rings." replied Don.

"Oh. Haven't read that one yet." said Corey.

Toby said, "Yeah. I was named after my mom's uncle. At least it's nothing as weird as what my dad wanted to name me. Cabot. Is that a weird first name or what?"

Don said, "Yeah. I guess so."

The band went over several older songs and a couple of new ones with Don. He wasn't a baritone like Ben. His voice was closer to Pete, Ben's brother's range. Don was as tall as Fred, but he was thin like Corey. There was always a smile on his face. Everyone seemed to like his personality and his vocals.

IT'S THE BASS PLAYER!

Even Birney warmed up to him somewhat. After practice they stood around talking for a while.

"My girlfriend should be here shortly. She works evenings at the Kwik Chek grocery store downtown." said Don.

"No kidding? That's where I work in the afternoons, when I get out of college classes. Who is she? I probably know her." said Toby.

"Well. Everyone else calls her Denise, but I call her by her middle name, Layla." answered Don.

"Yeah. I know Denise. She went to the county school. I think she was one of the majorettes for the band." said Toby.

"So Whata ya think guys? Is he an okay singer or what?" asked Fred.

"Okay Fred. We'll try him out and see how it goes." droned Birney. "I'm sure you two will go along with what Fred wants," Birney said to Corey and Toby.

"Well. If nothing else, we're holding to the basic formula. Four musicians and a lead singer." added Corey.

Don spoke up, "And if it's any consolation, I can play the tamborine. Hey. There's a couple of songs I'd like us to work up eventually. One by Cher. That Gypsies, Tramps and Thieves song. And that other song by Bonnie Tyler."

"Yeah. But those are songs sung by women. Why do you want to sing a song that's done from a woman's point of view?" asked Toby.

"I just thought it would be different to do something like that." answered Don.

Birney frowned and just mumbled, "Whatever. Is this guy weird or is it just me?"

After Don left, Corey turned to Toby and said, "Looks like we picked up a weirdo."

The next weekend the band played at Troy State in south Alabama. Fred had contacted his old football buddy, Carl

Bass, and had set up a gig at Carl's frat house. The frat house was rather large, as it used to be the hospital at one time. Don had brought two of his cousins with him. Dave and Dot Payton. Dave worked at the local radio station in Chalaka. He was on in the evenings on a program called "Music from beyond the Stars." He had replaced the original D.J. because his predecessor was bad about getting drunk on the air. The last night the previous D.J. was on, he had passed out with his microphone on. The record had played down to the end, and for a solid hour, All everyone could hear on their radios was the record skipping at the end and the D.J. snoring.So they had replaced the previous D.J. with Dave. But Dave was actually off this weekend, so Don had invited him and his sister to tag along.

The band had to rent a truck for this trip, since there weren't any trailers available. So all of the band except for Fred and Birney, rode in the back of the truck. Don had put a small mattress in the very back for everyone to sit on, since it was a good sized truck and all the equipment fit neatly in the front of the cargo area, which left plenty of room toward the back of the cargo area.

When they arrived at the frat house, Corey got out, took one look at the building, and said, "Hey Fred. Is somebody sick? This looks like a hospital, not a frat house. You sure we're at the right place? "

"Yup. This is the place. We're gonna play in the old operating room upstairs." replied Fred.

"Cool! So we're gonna perform musical surgery on our audience." quipped Corey.

Toby piped up, "Yeah. Give me a C note. Okay. Let's sew it up with this guitar string. Now give me an E flat. Never mind. Just give me an E and I'll flatten it."

IT'S THE BASS PLAYER!

Corey snickered, "I think the truck fumes have gotten to you Tobe."

That night before the band started, some of the frat guys had given everyone in the band a bottle of Cold Duck champagne a piece. Toby popped his cork first and tried a sip. "Man! This stuff is better'n seven up." he said between sips.

Corey warned, "You need to slow down on that stuff Tobe. You don't want to end up like Paul in Columbus."

"Yeah. You're right. It's one thing to not have a keyboard player, but we gotta have a bass player for the gig." said Fred.

"Okay. Okay. I'm slowin' down." grimaced Toby.

The band set up in the "operating room". It was an octagonally shaped room. The dance area was dead center of the room. There was a side room behind a door on the wall next to the hallway. That's where the frats set up the bar. The band played the first two sets without problems. Toby kept sipping on the Cold Duck between songs. On the second break, someone mounted a strobe light on the wall. When the band started their third set, someone turned on the strobe. Toby froze up. He couldn't play with the strobe in his eyes. He was afraid he was going to have a seizure because of the strobe. He pulled the microphone stand around facing Corey. In the middle of a song, Corey noticed Toby turned around facing him. He got concerned with the look on Toby's face.

Corey mouthed, "You okay?"

Toby shook his head no.

Corey mouthed, "What is it?"

Toby mouthed back, "The strobe."

At the end of the third set Toby went over to Fred and told him about the problem. Fred went over and asked his frat buddies to leave the strobe light off.

"Sure. No problem. We don't want the band members freaking out and not able to play." they said.

The fourth set went off without a hitch. Don held up pretty good all night. Even after downing a lot of liquor. The band packed up. Some of the frat guys helped them move and load the equipment. Dot and Dave Payton bragged on Don and the band on the way home until they went to sleep. Toby had fallen asleep ten minutes after they got on the road back home. They got back to Fred's and unloaded and went home.

They practiced Tuesday and Thursday night the following week. Don kept insisting on learning Gypsies, Tramps and Thieves by Cher, which the rest of the band just said no. Birney told the guys later that he thought Don had a screw loose. Fred had booked the band back at Troy State for the following weekend at a frat house there for a "Spooktacular Party". They worked up a couple of old tunes like the Monster Mash and Spooky by the Classics Four for the occasion. Corey and Toby were at the music store after practice discussing going in costumes.

"Well Corey. What would you go as?" asked Toby.

"What else? A crab. I could make some crab claws out of clorox bottles and duct tape and put a piece of poster paper on my back and front for my shell. Paint all of it red and wear my red turtle neck and red slacks. Then I'll really look like I'm cookin'! I bet I know what you'll be Tobe."

"Yeah? Who?" asked Toby.

"Well. Igor of course. Dr. Frankenstein's assistant." snickered Corey.

"Yeah. I'll paint up my face to look more distorted than usual, put a pillow on my shoulder, to give me the hunchback look, and borrow mom's wig. Wear some old raggity clothes. And There you'll have it. smiled Toby. "Oh yeah. You'll need some antennae for you head, Corey."

IT'S THE BASS PLAYER!

"Yeah. No problem. A coathanger bent just right will do." answered Corey. "Hey. I know the perfect costume for Fred. Stick a couple of fake bolts on his neck and paint him green, and he can be the Frankenstein monster." laughed Corey.

"Yeah. With that little bit of accessories, he'd be perfect." snickered Toby. "Only one problem with the crab suit though. Won't the crab claws get in the way when you try to play your drums?"

"Nah. I'll just tape 'em to my forearms, or better yet, put 'em on my shins so when I do the crab, my feet and legs will look like the claws." laughed Corey.

"That might work." smiled Toby.

Fred came up after talking to Don and said, "So what are you two talking about?"

"Next weekend. Since it is a spooky party, Toby and I are probably gonna dress up." answered Corey.

"Dressin' up for a spooky party is for kids. But then, you two are still kids at heart, I guess." said Fred.

"Well. Actually, I gave up my hotwheels years ago." smiled Corey. "Traded 'em in for Playboy." he said with a twinkle in his eye.

"I know what you guys were sayin' about me and Frankenstein. I'd prefer the Incredible Hulk. WAAAAH!" Fred said as he did his Hulk impression.

Corey snickered, "Yeah. But don't rip your pants off. We don't wanna run the audience off."

"Cute Corey." smiled Fred.

The weekend came and the guys loaded up and headed for Troy State once more. This time Fred had rented a trailer to pull behind his GTO. Don and Corey rode in Don's Oldsmobile four forty two. Fred, Toby, Birney, and Don's buddy, Corky Brown, rode in the GTO. Corky had a reputation as a professional drunk. Fred had hardly ever seen Corky sober. Corky's dad owned a tire business in town and Corky occasionally worked for his dad. Corky's wife worked at the Chalaka hospital on a different shift from Toby's mom.

When they pulled up in front of the frat house, Fred said, "Well guys. Welcome to the haunted funeral home frat house."

"You mean this used to be a funeral home? Cool! No better place to play for a spooky party guys!" smiled Corey.

"Yeah. Last week we played in the hospital. This week we're playing at a funeral home. Sounds like we're hittin' a dead end here, boys." drawled Birney.

Everyone snickered at Birney's dry humor. The band started unloading and moving the equipment into the old embalming room. It was the largest room in the building. The band got set up to play, got a sound check, and then went to relax for a while before playing. The frat guys had set up a huge buffet table, so Corey was the first one to hit the table. The rest of the guys came over and fixed themselves a plate of food. All except Corky, who was enjoying his buzz from his booze. Don got into the mixed drinks after they ate. By the time the band started their first set, Don was pretty well lit. By the second set he was very much wasted. Corey, Toby, and Fred had all dressed in their costumes for the gig. They fit in with the rest of the frat guys and their dates. Most of the frats had on costumes.

Before the band played the first set, Birney asked them "Well. What do y'all think about my costume?"

"You don't have a costume. What are you supposed to be?" asked Toby.

"Well, a hippy of course." answered Birney.

"And it's the perfect costume too." snickered Corey.

Into the third set, Don had gotten so drunk, he couldn't stand up and sing.

IT'S THE BASS PLAYER!

At one point, when the band was playing a love ballad, Corky got up in Fred's face, drunk as a skunk, yelling, "Y'all play somethin' wild! Y'all play somethin' wild!"

Fred just ignored him and went on playing. Corky then went staggering backwards and fell on one of the tables and knocked it over. Food and drinks went everywhere. Corky laid there in the floor passed out with booze and food all over him. Fred and Toby just rolled their eyes and kept on playing. After they got through playing, one of the frat guys took them on a tour of the "Haunted Basement". The frat guy talked about bringing dates down there and scaring the crap out of 'em. When they got through with the tour, they came upstairs to find Corky and Don both passed out on the dance floor. Fred, Corey, Toby and Birney packed up the equipment and loaded it back up. Toby volunteered to drive Don back to Chalaka. They piled Corky in the back seat of Fred's GTO and loaded Don in the passenger seat in his car.

About halfway back to Chalaka, Don woke up and said,"Uh. I'm gonna be sick."

With that, he hung his head out the window and threw up all over the side of his car. He then laid back in the seat and passed out again. He didn't move again until Toby and Fred and the band went by Don's apartment. Toby parked the car. The guys got Don and Corky out and helped tote them into Don's apartment. After they dropped Don and Corky off, they went back to Fred's, unloaded the equipment, and went home. It took almost a week to get all the green color off Fred's face and hands from his Incredible Hulk costume that he wore at the frat house. Wanda, the piano instructor at the store, teased Fred about being green around the gills almost all week. Jimmy Pope, the piano tuner, who was blind, kept teasing Fred too.

He would laughingly tell Fred when he would come in, "Well Fred, I SEE that you're still green with envy about my piano playing talent."

The following Monday, the band had a meeting without Don. Birney was very upset about Don getting too drunk to finish the show that Saturday night.

"We don't need a bunch of drunks raising hell and passing out when we play. I mean, if people in the audience get drunk and pass out, that's one thing. But we're being paid to entertain. Not raise hell and pass out." he said, "I vote we fire Don and just keep it four piece."

Fred and the rest of the band were upset about Don's shenanagans Saturday night. They voted with Birney on the termination of Don. Fred called Don the next day and told him the news.

"That's okay. I didn't care to play with a bunch of kids anyway. I'm good enough to go professional. So up yours Fred. And your band can stick it where it don't snow too." groused Don.

CHAPTER 14

More Changes and the Wreck

On Thursday, Fred got a phone call from Pete, Ben's brother.

"Hey. I'm back in town for a while Fred. And I was wondering if you guys are still playing."

Fred said, "Yup. We're still at it. We just fired our latest lead singer 'cause he got drunk and passed out at a frat party while we were still playin'." answered Fred.

"Are y'all still practicin' at your house on Tuesdays and Thursdays?" asked Pete.

"Nah. Since I've been working at the music store, we've been practicin' down there after hours." said Fred.

"Would y'all mind if I just came by and said hey one night?" asked Pete.

"You don't even have to ask that question Pete. You know you're welcome anytime." answered Fred.

That night Pete showed up at practice. Everybody greeted Pete cordially.

"You come back to pick with us Pete?" asked Corey.

"I just came by to holler at you boys, and see what's goin' on." answered Pete.

Even Birney was glad to see Pete.

"Are you guys still writin' tunes?" asked Pete.

Fred said, "Yup. You writin' anything Pete?"

Pete said, "Yeah. While I was at college I wrote a bunch of tunes."

Corey said, "Birney. What do ya think about Pete comin' back and singing with us again?" Birney smiled, "Well at least Pete has a professional attitude. Unlike the last drunk we hired."

"Yeah. I heard. Even brought his drunk sidekick with him. Fred told me they both passed out while you guys were playin.'" alleviated Pete.

"Yeah. Don was really good on the vocals, but he didn't know when to put the bottle down." added Fred.

"Well. Y'all know me. I'd rather split the money four ways instead of five, but, then, Pete was in the band before I was. And at least he's got a good attitude. So I guess we're back to five again. And at least he can play rhythm guitar." stated Birney.

The next day, Fred announced to the band that he contacted Hal Hodgins at Sound Of Birmingham recording studios, to record some new tunes. He and Toby were always writing new tunes, and Birney had written a few himself, so they were eager to go in a recording studio and put them down on tape. On Saturday morning, they loaded up the trailer again to go to Sound of Birmingham Studios.

Birney said, "So what's our motivation for spending money on this recording session again?"

Fred answered, "You know that Hal Hodgins is a D.J. at WVOK radio in Birmingham. Right? He told me if our songs are good enough, he'll play one of 'em on WVOK. He's trying to make a way for local bands to be heard."

Birney smiled, Sounds like a good motivation for investing in this adventure."

IT'S THE BASS PLAYER!

Corey looked up from the backseat and said, "Duh. What'd he say?"

Toby snickered, "He said okay. Let's do dis thing."

Corey just said, "Oh."

Corey played dumb at times, but his I.Q. was one hundred fifty. So he was no dummy. Fred, Corey, Toby, and Birney were riding in Fred's GTO that was pulling the Uhaul trailer, while Pete and his brother, Jerry, were following in Pete's Maverick. As Fred's car went over a bridge in Westover, that kind of dipped in the middle on this two-lane blacktop highway number 280 at sixty miles an hour, the trailer broke loose from the car. As Fred slowed down and hollered, "What the?"

They watched in horror and halfway amusement as the trailer passed them in the left lane and traveled another hundred yards. It then made a hard left, sailed off a six foot embankment, and landed upside down in the middle of a field of grass, next to a small pond. Fred slowed down and pulled into a dirt driveway just next to the small field. Toby jumped out of the window before Fred could stop, and ran down to the trailer. He reached to open the doors on the trailer, when he noticed a small snake come crawling out from under the trailer. He kicked the snake halfway across the field.

"No time for that." he muttered.

He went to pulling out the equipment and instruments. By this time, Corey was at his side, helping pull everything out.

When they had dragged everything out, Toby said, "Looks like the worst damage is the Hammond organ. Sorry Birney."

Corey had pulled his drums out and sat down on the ground after examining them.

"Man. My bass drum has a hole in it the size of Fred's ego." he muttered.

Toby and Corey examined each piece of equipment and instrument. Toby saw that his bass guitar case was cracked, but there wasn't a scratch on his bass. Everything else was okay. Fred went over to the house next to the field and called the Uhaul dealer in Chalaka. The Uhaul guy said he would send a wrecker to pick up the trailer and send a truck to pick up the equipment. Fred thanked him after giving him directions on where the trailer was. He went back out to the field and joined the guys. He told them someone was on the way.

"I don't think that guy put the trailer on the hitch right, Fred. And if there's anybody who knows trailer hitches, it's me." Toby grumbled.

Fred muttered, "I think you're right Tobe."

They turned to see a sports convertible pulling in behind Fred's car in the driveway. Fred recognized the guy getting out as one of his buddies that hung out at the Frosty Inn, Sniffy Gilbert.

He and his wife, Teresa, walked over and said, "I thought that was you Fred. Man. Y'all getting ready to have your own Woodstock out here? Need any help settin' up?"

Corey turned around and said, "No man! Our trailer just broke loose from the car and smashed up our equipment!"

"Oh. Sorry man. Anything we can do to help?" Sniffy apologized.

Toby said, "I guess we missed our appointment at the studio. Huh?"

Fred said, "Well. There'll be other times for that Tobe. I'm just glad nobody got hurt. That trailer could have slammed into the car when it passed us."

"Guess you're right. Well. Let's get this stuff ready to take home." answered Toby.

"If it's any consolation, Birney, if the keyboard will still play, I know a cabinet maker who can rebuild the frame, and maybe make it a little lighter too." said Fred.

IT'S THE BASS PLAYER!

The Uhaul truck showed up with the wrecker. As soon as they had loaded everything in the truck, they headed home with a load of discouragement. Luckily, they didn't have any bookings for that particular Saturday night. Corey had tinkered with the organ all day Sunday and declared it playable. None of the keys were cracked or broken. All of the electronics were intact. On Monday Fred called the cabinet maker to rebuild Birney's keyboard frame. Fred asked the cabinet maker if he could put a rush on it, so by Thursday the Hammond M series organ was ready. Corey had taken a staple gun and stapled the piece that had been busted in the side of his bass drum. He then used some industrial strength glue, and glued it in place. Toby's bass had a short in it from the wreck, but not enough to keep him from playing.

CHAPTER 15

The Place, Dating, and More Changes

Fred, Toby, and Corey met on a Thursday at Pasquale's downtown for supper. Gerald Crowe, the owner, came over and sat down with them.

"So what's our local celebrity band up to?" he asked.

"Just discussin' playin' a couple of proms. What's up with you Gerald?" asked Fred.

"Oh not much. I don't know if y'all have noticed, but I bought the place on the other side of the building." answered Gerald.

Corey spoke up, "Yeah. I did notice all the construction work goin' on over there. What are ya gonna put over there?"

Gerald smiled, "OH. Not much. Just a teen club, minus any alcohol. That's what I wanted to talk to you boys about. I need somebody to line up the bands to play over there. You guys have first choice of when you wanna play over there. Whata y'all think?" Fred smiled, "I think you've hit on a goldmine Gerald. I'll contact National Entertainment Agency in Atlanta, who we just hooked up with for bookings, and get them to send some bands when you get the place ready. What are you gonna call it?"

Gerald said, "I thought I'd leave it up to your brainpans."

Corey said, "You've already named it. The Place. It's the Place to be."

IT'S THE BASS PLAYER!

"The Place. I like that. It's got a ring to it." grinned Gerald. "Thanks guys. When

y'all get ready, I'll show y'all around over there." he said as he got up.

"That is so cool! There's finally a place for local bands like us to play without having to put up with a bunch of liquored up rednecks." said Corey.

"Hey. I don't mean to change the subject, but I heard from the folks at the Winterboro prom committee. They said the only way they would let us have the booking is if we're a mixed band. Toby, you being part Indian doesn't qualify." smiled Fred. "So I have an idea. There's a girl that's been coming in down at the music store. She sings like Diana Ross and kind of looks like her. I'll see if she wants to do the Winterboro prom with us." "Sounds good to me. The important thing is that she can sing well with the band. Right?" responded Toby.

The next day, Fred called Toby.

"Hey. We're gonna try out with Gwen McKelvey tomorrow night at the store."

"Who's that?" asked Toby.

"The girl I told y'all about at Pasquale's." answered Fred.

"Oh. Cool! Any idea what songs she's gonna sing?" asked Toby.

"Some of the tunes Donna sang, along with some Aretha Franklin and Dianna Ross tunes." answered Fred.

The band practiced the next night with Gwen and everyone was very pleased with the sound. Fred called the people back for the Winterboro high school prom committee and told them that the Common Faith was now a mixed band, and the playing price would have to go up slightly, since there were six members. They agreed and asked if Fred could send them some pictures of the group.

Fred said, "Sure. We might can have them to you as early as next week."

He called Toby and told him about the picture thing.

Toby said, "I know somebody who could take some pics of us, and I know just the place to take the shots. Simon Sandall can take them and we can take 'em at Bull Gap."

"I like that Idea Tobe. Let's do it." said Fred.

"Consider it a done deal." answered Toby.

Toby called Corey and informed him of the photo shoot.

All Corey said was, "Here we go again."

"Think about it this way Corey. As long as you, me, Fred and Birney keep on playin' together, then there's always gonna be a Common Faith. The Donnas, Gwens, Bens,Pauls, and Petes may come and go, but we'll keep on hangin' in there like a rusty nail." countered Toby.

"Okay. You're right. I'm done with all that jinx jazz." sighed Corey in relief.

The following saturday the band rode out to Bull Gap in the Talladega National Forest. The gap sat on the side of a mountain east of Chalaka. There were some very large exposed rocks above the dirt road that went down the side of the mountain off of the main highway. The band sat on top of the rocks and posed while Mr. Sandall stood down on the road snapping pictures. When he was finished, he told them the pictures would be ready Monday.

"That quick?" asked a surprised Fred.

"Yeah. I've got my own darkroom for developing pictures." answered Mr. Sandall. Fred delivered the pictures and business cards to the committee at Winterboro on Tuesday. The committee was unanimous about the Common Faith playing at their prom. Fred came back with the booking for the prom.

IT'S THE BASS PLAYER!

The band played the Winterboro prom. Gwen added a new sound to the group. Eveyone really liked the way the band sounded. On the third break of the show, several girls approached the guys.

A very cute girl with short brown hair spoke up,"Hi. We were wondering if you guys could help us out. Our dates stood us up for the prom, and we don't have anybody to take Pictures with. We were wondering if some of y'all would mind having your picture made with us."

Corey beamed, "Well of course! We would love to take pictures with you lovely ladies. I'm Corey Gable, this is Toby Martin, Pete Regis, and that's Fred Litton and the guy who just went outside is Birney Peters."

"I'm Sally Killough, this is Nancy Quebec, Jane Watts, Janis Poore, and Joan Nielson." said Sally.

Jane came over to Corey and said, "Would you mind having your picture taken with me? The jerks that were supposed to be our dates stood us all up because they all wanted to go get drunk or high or something."

"I would love to have such a lovely lady on my arm." smiled Corey.

Nancy piped up, "Hey! I saw him first."

Jane smiled back, "Sorry Nancy. You snooze, you lose."

Sally turned to Toby and said, "Would you take a picture with me?"

Toby smiled, "Yes. I would love to with a pretty lady like you."

Joan looked at Pete and said,"Well. What do ya think?"

Pete said, "Sounds okay to me."

Janis gave Fred the once-over. "Okay big boy. Looks like it's you and me."

Fred just nodded and grinned.

Nancy whined, "Hey. what about me? There's nobody left for me. And your keyboard player went outside, so I can't ask him."

Toby piped up, "I'm sorry. Hey. I don't mind having my picture made with you and Sally both in it. How about it?"

Sally said, "Yeah Nancy. You are my best friend. I don't mind sharing a picture with the three of us in it."

Nancy stopped pouting and said, "Okay. But this will cost Toby there a yankee dime." Toby scratched his head and said, "A what?"

Nancy walked over to Toby, wrapped her arms around his waist and said, "I'll show you."

She then kissed Toby full on the lips. She leaned back.

Toby could only mumble, "Whuh.whuh.whuh."

"That's the first time I've known Tobe to be short on words." snickered Corey.

Sally said, "Well. Let's make it a double shot."

She pushed Nancy back, grabbed Toby by the collars and planted another big smooch on him.

All Toby could say when she released him was, "Wooooah!"

Jane looked at Corey and said, "Sorry. I don't kiss on the first date."

Corey said, "No problem. I take it you value yourself as a lady. If that's the case, you'll be treated with that respect."

Jane said, "Thank you Sir Corey. Then I'll be your lady in waiting for now." as she curtseyed as though she were bowing before royalty.

Corey bowed from the waste and said, "Thank you ever so much milady."

Sally said, "Well, Toby, looks like you'll be taking a picture with this brunette on one arm and that blonde on the other." as she pointed at Nancy.

IT'S THE BASS PLAYER!

Toby grinned and said, "Man. I'll feel like a best selling novel with you two lovely ladies on my arm."

Nancy said, "Yeah. And with that big sleeved, open collared shirt you have on, I feel like I'm in a picture with Tom Jones."

Everyone had their pictures made. Corey with Jane. Toby with Sally and Nancy. Pete with Joan. And Fred with Janis. Birney had not cared to have his picture made with anybody. As he said, it was beneath him. After the picture sessions, the band got back on stage for one last set.

Jane kept swooning, "OOOOH Corey!" which lit Corey up like a roman candle.

Toby and Nancy kept winking back and forth at each other.

After the band finished their last song and started breaking down, Sally and Nancy came up to Toby and said, "We're having a party at my house after this. Would y'all like to come?"

Toby said, "It all depends. See? We've got to take our equipment back to Chalaka and unload it. Then we can come back up here for the party. I just hope it'll still be goin' on when we get there. And we need directions how to get there."

Sally said, "If YOU'RE coming, we'll keep it goin till you get there."

Sally gave Toby directions to her parent's house.

Toby smiled, "Okay, But there's one condition to this invite."

Sally looked puzzled and said, "What's that?"

Toby smiled, "It will cost Nancy there another yankee dime."

Nancy rushed over to Toby and said, "Is that all? You can have a hundred dollars worth." She grabbed Toby. Toby wrapped his arms around her and bent her over backwards while kissing her on the lips.

Sally just said, "Boy. You put Rhett Butler to shame with that one."

Nancy and Toby stood there looking into each other's eyes for a few minutes. The rush slowly faded and they released each other hesitantly.

Sally grabbed Nancy's arm and said, "Come on. They've got to finish loading up so they can make it to the party."

Toby smiled an ear to ear grin and said, "I'll see you shortly princess."

She smiled back and could only say "Okay."

Fred said, "You can count me and Pete in too for the party."

Jane came over to Corey and took his hand in hers, and said, "I won't be going to Sally's party. My parents won't let me stay out that late."

"Well. Can I get your phone number, so I can call you tomorrow?" asked Corey.

"Yes. Of course, Sir Corey." answered Jane.

She wrote her number down and gave it to Corey. When she handed him the note, she took both his hands and said, "I guess I kind of lied about that first kiss thing."

Corey smiled, leaned to her and kissed her long.

All the other girls were going, "OOOOH Corey!"

Jane whispered, "Goodnight Sir Corey."

Corey bowed from the waste once more and said, "Goodnight milady."

The band packed up and headed back to Chalaka to unload their equipment in the back of the teen club next to Pasquale's, since they were scheduled to play there the following weekend. Gerald, the owner, had left the back door key with Fred for that purpose.

As they were unloading, Toby asked, "So are you going to Sally's party, Corey?"

"Nah. I think I'll just go on home." answered Corey.

"You oughta go with me. Hey. Maybe your new girlfriend will be there." offered Toby. "First of all, she's not my girlfriend, yet. And I know she won't be there because her parents won't let her stay out late. So I'm just goin' on home. I did get her phone number though." answered Corey.

Toby went on to the party with Fred and Pete and paired up with Nancy. Sally's boyfriend showed up for the party, which made her happy. Fred and Pete paired up with Janis and Joan at the party. They stayed and partied till the wee hours in the morning there at Sally's parent's house next to the pond. Corey went home. He called Jane the next day for a date to go to the movies the following Thursday night.

Two weeks later, on that Friday night, the band played at the Village Square Club, opening for a new band called the Georgia Satellites. Then Saturday night they were in a small town ninety miles north of Mobile called Grove Hill. Gwen had decided she didn't care for all the traveling that the band did, so on Saturday morning she had told Fred that she quit. Corey's mom, Gladys, had gone with the band to Atlanta Friday, because Gwen's parents had insisted that there be an adult to chaperone, since none of the band members were over twenty. Toby was glad that Corey's mom, Gladys, had volunteered to go with them on that Friday night. He enjoyed being around Corey's mom because she had that same spark of humor that Corey had. Toby always thought it was an inherited trait. Pete had started dating Joan and decided that the band was taking up too much of his time that he could be spending with Joan. So he had called Fred and told him that he quit. So that Saturday night the band was back to four members again. The guys seemed to be getting used to constant changes in personnel. They knew as long as the four of them hung in there, that there would always be a Common Faith.

Tuesday, Fred went to work at the store, and met a guy from Alexander City named Mike Hammond who played guitar. Mike had played with a band that had a shot at a recording contract and touring with some big name acts. The band had broke up before they could be signed though. So Mike was looking for another band. Fred invited Mike to come jam with his band there at the store the next night. The band jammed the next night with Mike. Birney and Mike hit it off great. Corey and Toby enjoyed playing with him too.

When the jam was over, Fred said, "What do you guys think?"

Birney, Corey, and Toby were all saying, "Welcome to the Common Faith."

Fred asked, "You guys sure about this? I mean. Granted, we can do any Allman Brothers tune, or any other heavy rock tune, but are y'all sure?"

"Yeah. You okay with it Fred?"asked Corey.

Fred said, "Sounds okay to me. Welcome to the band Mike."

"Thanks guys." answered Mike.

The band played at the Place the next weekend. All the local kids bragged on how much better the band sounded with a second guitar. Mike seemed to fit in like he had played with the band for years.

CHAPTER 16

Groupy Problems and Cutting a Record

Monday, Mike decided to call a friend of his in Muscle Shoals to set up an auditioning recording session at Muscle Shoals Recording Studio. The studio where a lot of famous acts had recorded. He scheduled a session for the following Sunday. since the band was slated to play in a small town called Catherine at the high school the upcoming Saturday night. He called the rest of the guys and told them the news about the studio. They had written seven new songs. They practiced on the songs twice that week. The guys were ready for the weekend by Thursday. The band played for a prom Friday night in Weogufka. With the exception of some girl trying to jump Fred's bones, as she put it, the night was uneventful. They played their four sets, finished up, and broke down to go. Fred had to hide out in the trailer and load equipment, so the girl that was hot after him wouldn't find him. They loaded up and left. Saturday afternoon they headed to Catherine, Alabama. They got there at about six p.m. They set up in the old high school auditorium on stage and played that night. On each break, several girls kept hanging around the band and talking to Fred and the guys. Mike was quick to inform them that he was married, so the girls mostly talked to Toby, Corey, Fred, and Birney. One girl named Sandra kept trying to corner Toby in a dark spot backstage, but Toby was uneasy, not knowing how old she was. Since all the guys in the band were nineteen or a little younger, any girl under fifteen was off limits in their opinion. What they called "jail bait". Too young to mess with or date. When they finished playing that night, the band was hauling the equipment out to the trailer. Toby was carrying some of Corey's drums out and putting them in the trailer. He had stepped up into the front of the trailer and bent over to put the hardware in place. About that time someone closed the door on the back of the trailer. He could tell there was someone in the trailer with him, even though it was pitch dark. He suddenly felt a female body pressing against him. He felt her arms circling his neck.

A soft voice said, "It's me Sandra. I want you."

Then he felt her lips on his.

He backed up as much as he could and said, "Look. You're cute and all, but, just how old are you?"

She said, "I'm seventeen."

Toby tensed and asked again, "How Old?"

"Okay. Fifteen. But that doesn't matter. Does it?" She asked as she tried to kiss him again.

He scooted around her and pushed the trailer door open. Corey was coming out to the trailer with a speaker cabinet.

He saw Toby, then saw Sandra behind him and said, "Shame shame. I know your name." Toby turned to Sandra and said, "Look. If you want to be my pen pal, that's fine. That way we can get to know each other, but I'll just tell you like it is. I don't play kiss and hug, and I certainly don't date any girl under sixteen. So if you want to wait a couple of years to take up where we left off just now, that'd be fine. But not now."

"Okay. So you want my address and maybe give me yours?" she asked pouting.

That's okay with me." smiled Toby.

IT'S THE BASS PLAYER!

They swapped addresses. Sandra tried to hug Toby again, but he shook her hand and said, "Don't forget to write."

He then went to hauling equipment back out to the trailer. When Toby went into the auditorium to bring out another piece of equipment, he asked Fred, "What is it? A full moon this weekend? First the Sheila girl was trying to jump your bones last night, as she put it, and now this girl going after me tonight. I wouldn't have minded as much if she'd been seventeen at least, but I don't date jail bait."

"I don't know Tobe. That girl last night was old enough, but she had a green cloud following her around." answered Fred.

"What do you mean a green cloud?" asked Toby.

"Pardon my French, but she smelled like one big fart." explained Fred.

Toby burst out laughing. "Yeah. I'd say that's a good reason to avoid somebody. When someone's breath smells like their other end, it's time to go."

"It wasn't just her breath. Her body odor smelled like farts, moth balls,and bad perfume. And while she was talking to me, she pooted twice, loudly. I guess she thought that would turn me on or something."

Toby chuckled, "Err. Thats a really bad combination, Fred."

Mike brought out the last of the equipment and said, "Allright fellas. Let's close her up and head north."

They closed up the trailer. Fred, Corey, and Toby got in the GTO and Mike and Birney got in Mike's Plymouth Satellite. The trip to Muscle Shoals was uneventful until they got to Hamilton, Alabama, which was thirty miles from Muscle Shoals. As they passed the city limits sign to Hamilton, a police car pulled in behind them and turned on his blue lights.

Fred said, "What the? What's this all about?"

Toby woke up and looked back. "What's goin' on Fred?" he asked.

Fred pulled over and said, "I have no idea, Tobe. I know I wasn't speeding."

The police officer came up to Fred's window and said, "Would you step out of the car please."

Fred stepped out and handed the officer his Driver's license. "What's this all about officer?" he asked.

"Mr. Litton. Would you mind opening your trailer and letting me see what you're hauling? We've had a problem in our dry county with bootleggers bringing in liquor from out of the county." stated the officer.

Sure. No problem. We're in a band, on our way to Muscle Shoals to do some recording from Catherine, Alabama." explained Fred, as he walked back to the trailer with the officer.

Fred opened the trailer and the policeman shined his light inside.

"Okay. Looks fine to me." He handed Fred his driver's license. "You boys be careful on the road." he said.

"Thank you officer." replied Fred.

He got back in the car and drove on to Muscle Shoals.

The band checked into a motel near the river in Muscle Shoals. After catching a few hours sleep, Fred and the band drove to Fame Recording Studio. Fred and Mike got out and knocked on the door.

Rick Hall answered the door and said, "What can I do for you fellas?"

Mike spoke up, "Hey Rick. It's me. Mike Hammond. My band, Powacket, came in and recorded with you last year."

Rick grabbed Mike's hand and shook it. "Oh yeah. Hey! Great to see you Mike. I meant to call and find out how things went after your session here with Burkett handling the A&R."

Mike said, "Not too well. After we recorded our album, one of the guys decided to quit, so we lost our contract. This is Fred Litton. I'm playing with his band now. We're up here to record an audition session with Barry over at MSS."

"Great! It's good to see you again. I was baby sitting a session with some guys, if y'all would like to watch for a little while, you're more than welcome." smiled Rick.

"Yeah. We can stay a little while. Who ya got in there?" asked Mike.

"Oh. Steve Winwood and Traffic. Their wrapping up their final tracks now." answered Rick. "Who's the rest of your crew here?"

Mike said, "Oh. I'm sorry. You've met Fred. This is Toby, Birney, and Corey."

Rick smiled, "Nice to meet you boys. Come on in and take a load off. We've got food in the little kitchen there, and cokes if you're thirsty. Just make yourselves at home."

They came in and sat in front of a window facing the performance room, and watched Traffic record their tracks. Traffic didn't come out of the performance room to greet the guys, as they were intent on getting their album finished. While the guys were watching Traffic record, Fred and Mike went in the engineer booth and talked to Rick Hall. Birney was focused on every note that Steve Winwood played and sang. After a while, Fred and Mike came out of the engineering room.

Fred said, "You guys about ready to head over to Muscle Shoals Sound?"

Birney turned and said, "Man. I hate to leave here. I've learned a few things just sitting here watching Steve."

Rick walked in and said, "Do you guys want to meet Steve and the band before you leave?"

Fred and the guys said, "Yeah. Sure!"

Rick went back in the booth and called out to the guys in Traffic over the intercom, "Hey guys. Could you take a break for a second and come in here? I've got somebody who wants to meet ya."

They all said, "Sure." and came in the break room.

The two bands met and exchanged pleasantries.

Steve Winwood asked Birney, "So. Are you guys gonna record here with Rick?"

Birney grinned, "Nah. We've got an appointment over at Muscle Shoals Sound today." "Oh. Well. If you guys ever want to work with the best, Rick's your man." Steve said. Birney replied, "Cool. Well it was great to meet y'all. I know y'all wanna get back to recording."

Steve said,"Likewise. Good luck over at MSS."

Birney and the band thanked everyone, shook hands and left. They drove over to Muscle Shoals Sound, got out and went in. The outside of the building looked run down and uncared for, but the inside was immaculate.

The receptionist said when they came in, "Can I help you gentlemen?"

Mike replied,"Yes. I'm Mike Hammond and…"

"Oh. Mr. Hammond. Yes. Mr. Burkett is expecting you." she interupted with a smile. "One moment and I'll let him know you're here."

The secretary pressed the intercom switch and said,"Mr. Burkett, Mr. Hammond is here.A voice came from the back of the room, "No need in hollerin' on that thing, I can hear you just fine." said Barry Burkett as he came in the room.

He was a rather rotund, blonde headed, bespectacled man with an ever present smile on his face. Mike went through the Introductions of the band. Barry had the studio ready to record. He put everyone in their own little booth with their instruments and vocal mics. When Barry took Corey over to the drum booth, Corey said, "I hope you've got a headset with decent volume controls."

IT'S THE BASS PLAYER!

Barry smiled and asked, "Why is that?"

"Because the last time we went in a studio, the volume control on my headset didn't work. The volume was all the way up, and Fred there, almost deafened me with his loud guitar." stated Corey.

Barry laughed, "Okay. We'll make sure you have some excellent phones. And we'll filter Fred's guitar to blend. How about that?"

Fred smiled and muttered, "It wasn't that bad. Hey Tobe. You got any guitar picks? I forgot to bring any."

Toby smiled, "Now you know I've always got a pocket full of picks."

As Toby went over to the bass booth, he noticed many gold albums all over one wall. He noticed one that had the Rolling Stones' Sticky Fingers album label on it. There were gold albums from about every type of music played on the radio. Barry had worked with everybody in the music business who was anybody. Barry had been the keyboard player for a group of studio musicians called the "Swampers", which are mentioned in the song, Sweet Home Alabama. The Common Faith laid down tracks to seven songs that they wrote. After they finished putting down the tracks, Barry mixed them down and played them back one by one. He listened to about one to two minutes of each song.

After listening to these tidbits on the first six songs, he said, "That don't hit me." after every song.

When he got to the seventh song, which Toby, Fred and Birney wrote together, and Birney sang, he sat and listened intently to the whole song.

"I think we've got something here." he finally said.

He backed it up and listened to the whole song again.

After listening to the whole song again, he looked up over his glasses and said, "I believe you boys have hit on something here. I love that accordion part you put in there Toby. You wouldn't want to sell that accordion would you?"

Toby shook his head, "Nah. It belonged to my dad. I couldn't part with it."

"Well. Let's go back and do an extremely professional cut on this song, and that "Thinking Thinking" song for a "B" side cut."

Corey jumped up and exclaimed, "Man! You mean we're goin' to actually cut a single? FAR OUT!"

They went back and recorded the two songs.

After they finished recording, Barry said, "Now that we've got a potential hit, one other thing. The band's name. It's not catchy enough. I would suggest another name, like Johnny Flash. And instead of calling the song just a "Beautiful Song", why not call it "I Can See Clearly"? And don't worry about the copyright on the song. We'll take care of it on this end."

Fred said, "Well. Since you've been in the business a while and know what you're doin', okay."

Barry said, "Great. I'll negotiate with one of the record labels and see what I can come up with."

Fred interjected, "Yeah. But we've still got several bookings contracted under the Common Faith name."

"That's fine. Whatever you guys need to do." said Barry.

Fred asked Barry if he could run off a copy of the songs, but Barry said he couldn't do that

"If you guys go out and release this to the public before we release it from here, we'd have all kinds of hell to pay from our lawyers." answered Barry.

"Well. I guess that's understandable." Muttered Fred. Everybody thanked Barry

for everything, got back in their vehicles, and headed back to Chalaka.

CHAPTER 17

Truck Troubles, Record Problems, and the Date

The next weekend the guys played at one of the frat houses at the University Of Alabama in Tuscaloosa Friday. Mr. Nelson, the man that owned the store that Fred worked at, let them use the company truck to haul their equipment. They got to the frat house that evening. Fred noticed that the temperature guage was all the way over in the red when he parked it.

"We may have a problem guys. Look at the temp gauge." he said.

"That's not good. We may have a leak in the radiator Fred." said Birney.

"You may be right. But let's get set up to play. We'll worry about that when we get through." answered Fred.

They set up and played. The frat members and their dates were singing along with the band on almost everything they sang. One girl that wasn't with anybody in particular came over to Birney when they were setting up and started talking to Birney. She had long brown hair almost the same length as Birney's. She stayed over by Birney's keyboard all night. She kept bringing Birney drinks when he'd finish his previous drink. Birney was beaming all night long. After the last song, she came over and sat down in his lap and whispered something in his ear.

Birney turned to the rest of the guys, who were breaking down the equipment, and said,"Hey guys. We'll be back shortly. I'm going to escort this lovely young lady out to her car."

Toby, Corey, and Fred smiled at each other, knowing what that meant.

Corey said after they walked out, "Birney's gonna get some sugar."

Toby smiled, "Yup. I think you're right."

When Birney came back, they packed up and loaded up the truck. The guys were teasing Birney about the nice shade of lipstick he was wearing.

Corey said, "Hey Birney. You need to get the big red smear off your neck too."

Birney smiled, "Ah. You guys are just jealous because you didn't have your main squeezes here. Think I'll bring this one home to meet momma soon."

They got in to go. Fred turned the starter switch and nothing happened.

"No! Not again! I am so sick of these vehicle problems!" he yelled.

Birney wiped the lipstick off his cheek and volunteered, "I'll go call a mechanic."

Fred said, "No. I'm gonna call Mr. Nelson and let him worry about this truck. Then we'll go get a UHaul truck and go home."

Fred did exactly that. He called Mr.Nelson, who sent a tow truck to pick up the company truck and had it towed back to Chalaka. Then Fred got one of the guys from the frat house to drive him to the local Uhaul dealer. They put their equipment in the rental truck and went home. Saturday afternoon they were on their way to Atlanta again, to play at a club down on Peachtree Street called Shananigan's. They played that night with no problems. On the second break Fred met a guy at the bar who was the manager for Gilbert O'Sullivan, who later became known as another one-hit-wonder with his song, "Alone Again Naturally". The manager invited Fred to a party at the hotel where Gilbert O'Sullivan and Three Dog Night were staying. Three Dog Night was playing that night with three or four other big name groups, including Gilbert O'Sullivan, at Atlanta's football stadium. Three Dog Night always had a party after they played large venues."Sure. I'd like to go, but can I bring a couple of the guys from the band with me?" asked Fred.

The manager said, "Well. I can only bring one guest. I'll leave it up to you. It could help your group get to that next level. You never know."

Fred grinned, "Okay. Count me in."

Fred went back to the table where the rest of the band was sitting.

"What's up Fred? You look like the cat that just swallowed the proverbial canary." said Mike.

"I just got invited to go to Three Dog Night's after gig party." grinned Fred.

"Wow! Cool. So where are we goin' for this party?" asked Corey.

"Well. That's the catch. Only one of us can go with that guy sitting at the end of the bar. He's the manager for Gilbert O'Sullivan."

Everybody chimed in, "Alone again, Naturally."

"Yeah. That guy. He's opening for Three Doggy tonight here in Atlanta." answered Fred.

"And I got a pretty good idea who that "one of us" is gonna be. Fred. I know this might help us in the long run, but there's more to this band than one guy on a guitar. You need to include the rest of us in on your negotiations and schmoozing." said Mike with a slightly sharp tone.

"I AM thinkin' of you guys. My whole purpose for attending this party is to push US up the ladder. Look. I promise I won't be gone long. I'll meet you guys back at Biscayne Heights, where we're staying tonight. Okay?" answered a slightly flustered Fred. "Allright. But I still think you could've squeezed me in on your little party plans." growled Mike.

Toby muttered to Corey, "He's starting to sound like a frustrated housewife."

Corey answered in a low voice, "Yeah. Looks like we got too many chiefs and not enough Indians."

Mike turned and said, "You say something Corey?"

Corey just said, "I was telling Toby that I hope it doesn't rain tonight when we load up." Mike just said, "Oh."

The band went back on stage and played their last two sets. They loaded up and headed over to Biscayne Heights apartment complex, where Mike knew the manager, Phillip Morris. Phillip let them stay in one of the half empty apartments free for the night. The band sat and waited for Fred, making idle chit chat while they waited. Fred came in around three.

Corey said, "So what's the news, Fred? Didja schmooze into the right groove?"

Fred grinned from ear to ear. "Boys. Looks like we're gonna be opening for Three Dog Night in Birmingham next Month!"

They all started chattering at once excitedly.

"That quick? You talked them into it that quick?" Corey stammered.

"Yup. All I had to do was talk to the manager, and tell him about our record that's coming from Muscle Shoals. When I mentioned Barry's name, it was like I turned on a switch." answered Fred.

"So are we Common Faith or Johnny Flash?" asked Toby.

IT'S THE BASS PLAYER!

"Well I told him we are Common Faith for now, but when the record comes out we will be Johnny Flash. He said he would go ahead and book us under our current name." said Fred.

"Great! that means I don't have to change any of the band logo tee shirts I had printed up."said Corey grinning.

"What tee shirts?" asked Fred.

"Just kidding. But it would be nice to have some tee shirts with our band name on 'em." answered Corey.

Mike pouted, "I still think you could've taken me with ya."

"Sorry Mike. But I was lucky to get to go at all. It was either me or that blonde that guy was checkin' out at the other end of the bar at Shananagin's. Luckily she didn't wanna go." stated Fred.

The band slept until nine the next morning. They got up and put on their shorts, and jumped into the pool at the complex.

As Corey, Fred, and Toby walked out to the pool, Corey called out, "Look out ladies. Here comes Corey the Crab, Gorilla man and the white Hulk."

Corey intoduced himself to a female airline attendant who was sunning herself by the pool. He spent the rest of his time there flirting with this girl.

Toby looked over at Corey and said "Shame shame. I know your name."

They dove in and swam in the pool for a couple of hours before they headed back home.

The following Monday, Toby came in from work at the local Kwik Chek, where he was a stock clerk/ grocery bag boy.

Louise called out from the kitchen,"Toby. You've got some mail on the TV there from Catherine, Alabama. Who do you know way down there?"

Toby said, "Oh. Some girl that I met when we played down there last weekend. She wanted us to be pen pals or something. I'll get it."

He opened the letter, which smelled of perfume, and started reading. It was from Sandra, the girl who tried to corner Toby at the gig in Catherine, Al. The letter mostly said how much she thought Toby was so good looking and how she wanted to come see him or for him to come get her and bring her to Chalaka. She also talked about how bad things were with her parents and how she wanted to get away from them. This threw up a red flag with Toby. He knew this girl was only fifteen and just going through that rebellious stage that all teens go through at that time. He had done his share of rebelling against his mom during his earlier teen years. But he knew this girl spelled trouble with a capital T. He sat down and wrote her a letter back and explained that he was now dating someone steady and that he wasn't interested in a long distance relationship, and on top of that, she was too young for him. He told her that the band probably wouldn't be coming back down that way for a long time. Toby didn't really know this for sure, but he figured she wouldn't know the difference. He told her if she wanted to write to him occasionally, that would be okay, but he wasn't interested in any romantic involvement with anyone else right now. He had found someone, and she was what he was looking for. He signed it, Your chordial friend, Toby.

On Tuesday, Fred called Toby, who was at Corey's that afternoon.

"Tobe. I just thought I'd give you the news first about Mike"

"Let me guess. He quit." surmised Toby.

"Yup. He wanted to be the leader of the band, since he was our contact with Barry. He didn't like me goin' over his head, as he put it, booking us with Three Dog Night." alleviated Fred.

IT'S THE BASS PLAYER!

"Guess Corey was right about too many chiefs and not enough Indians." smiled Toby. Fred snickered, "Yeah. I guess he was right."

Toby asked, "So what do we do now Fred?"

Fred answered, "Relax. I'll call Birney and tell him. He said he didn't care for Mike's attitude anyway. He said he'd call Johnny Pate and see if he'd like to play in Mike's place if we wanted him to. I think we're gonna take off this comin' weekend. It'll give us time to, uh, regroup."

"I'm glad to hear that Fred, cause Corey and I were talking about a double date with Nancy and Jane." smiled Toby.

Fred said, "Yeah. I got a date with Lorene Landers. She's got a twin sister, if you're interested, Tobe."

"No thanks. I'm a one woman man. I don't believe in dating more than one girl at a time. My little pea brain can't deal with more than one girl at a time." answered Toby.

He changed the subject.

"I've got to see about buying me another car sometime soon. The GTX is drinking way too much gas for my taste."

Fred said, "Yeah. With a four twenty six hemi engine with two four barrels, you can probably get to Childersburg and have to refill the tank."

Toby said, "I think I found me a nineteen sixty four Ford Galaxy station wagon. I'm goin' to check on it this weekend. Let me know what the verdict is on Johnny Pate. I'll tell Corey the news about Mike. Talk to ya later man."

Fred said, "Okay Tobe. Later."

Fred then called Barry Burkett and told him about Mike leaving the group.

"Well. I hate to say it, but without Mike, the deal will have to be postponed. We can't have a record going out there when one of your members isn't playing with the band anymore." said Barry.

"Can't you just pull his guitar track off?" asked Fred. "Besides, we've got another guitar player to replace him."

Barry replied, "That's hard to do, since I've already mixed it down. Especially since Atlantic specified Mike in the contract. Everyone's name and signature has to be on the contract. I was about to send you a copy for all you guys to sign. Now I can't. I'm sorry Fred. You guys would have to come back up here and recut the songs, then I'd have to renegotiate with the label for a new contract, and you would have to assure me that nobody else would quit. In short, it's more trouble than it's worth to me."

"Fred said, "I'm sorry you feel that way Barry."

Barry replied, "I hate it too. But that's just the way it is in this business."

Fred thought for a minute and said, "Is there any way we can come back up there and recut the song?"

Barry said, "Tell you what. You call me back in six months. If you guys are still together with the SAME people, I'll reschedule a new session to recut the song. But not any sooner. Okay?"

Fred acquiesced, "Okay. I'll be calling you back in six months then. Talk to ya then Barry. And thanks for every thing."

Barry came back, "NO problem Fred. See ya soon."

Corey and Toby went on their double date with Nancy and Jane on Saturday night. They went to the movies at Eastwood mall in Birmingham. After the movies the four decided to go through the drive thru at Kelly's Hamburgers, that was located in the parking lot at Eastwood Mall. Before they got to the driveway, Corey had Toby pull the GTX over.

"What are ya gonna do Corey?" asked Toby.

IT'S THE BASS PLAYER!

"Watch this." said Corey.

Nancy said, "Uh oh. Famous last words of a redneck."

Corey climbed out of the car and up on the hood of the car right in front of Toby and got into his famous crab position. He told Toby to pull up to the speaker to order the food. Everybody already knew what they wanted, so they pulled up to the speaker. A very nasal voice came over the speaker, which sounded like a voice through a tin can.

"Can I help you?"

Corey piped up in a crazy voice and said, "Ye daga doo blip blargle yetee gurgle ya hurly hurly hurly yo diggity blip blip blip."

Toby and the girls were dying laughing at Corey's antics.

The nasal voice said, "I'm sorry. What was your order again?"

Toby said, "He'll have a burger basket and a coke, and we'll have three more of the same."

The nasal voice came back and said, "So that'll be four burger baskets and four cokes?" Corey piped up again, "Ne tranga banga nui nui bleeka bleeka harip!"

Toby said, "He said that is Correct."

Toby and the girls were laughing so hard, their sides were hurting. Toby pulled up to the first window, so the girl taking the money couldn't see Corey on the hood. Toby paid for the food. Then they pulled up to the second window even with Corey on the hood. The girl didn't look out the window at first, but handed the bag full of burgers and fries out the window. Corey reached over and grabbed the bag in his teeth as he growled at her. The girl turned and screamed. Corey sat there and growled at her. Toby got out of the car, picked Corey up, who was still in the crab position, and put him in the backseat with Jane, while Corey still had the bag of food between his teeth. Toby came back over to the speechless girl and picked up the tray of drinks at the window.

He said, "Sorry. He just gets that way when he hasn't had his medication."

Toby got back in the car and drove away, leaving the girl in shock and awe.

As they pulled off, Corey said, "Hey. Can we do that again?"

Toby laughed, "Nah. It wouldn't be the same. They'd know what to expect."

As they parked on the other side of the parking lot and ate their meals, Jane turned to Corey and said, "I brought some peppermints in my purse in case we ate some onions on our burgers or whatever, just in case there was to be any kissing going on."

She looked Corey in the eye and said, "Well. This is our second date so…"

Corey said, "Yeah. And…? Oh!"

He reached over to kiss Jane.

She said, "I meant after we get through eating."

Corey backed up and said, "Oh. Okay."

They finished eating and headed to take the girls home. Corey and Jane were in a lip lock in the backseat, so things were quiet from them. Toby and Nancy talked about everything imaginable on the way back. Toby was grateful the car had power steering because he didn't want to let go of Nancy's hand for one second. Toby took Jane home, then Corey. Then he took Nancy to her house in Winterboro. He had her home before eleven o'clock, which was her curfew.

As he parked the car, Nancy said, "Thanks for a great time. I really enjoyed the movie, but I enjoyed the company more."

Toby smiled, "I'm glad you did."

He got out, came around and opened the car door for her and said, "I'll walk you to the door."

IT'S THE BASS PLAYER!

They walked to the door and Toby leaned over and kissed Nancy on the lips. She kissed him back.

When they drew back, she mumbled, "It's about freakin' time. I didn't think you were ever goin' to make your move."

Toby grinned back, "Well. Next time, if I don't make my move soon enough, you can make it for me."

At that, Nancy reached over and grabbed Toby by the collar and planted a big smooch on him.

When she pulled back she said, "Is that soon enough?"

"Not soon enough for me." said Toby as he kissed her again.

About that time the front porch light went on and Nancy's dad said from behind the door, "Daughter, time to come in."

She said, "Okay dad. I'm just saying goodnight to Toby." She turned to Toby and said, "Call me tomorrow."

Toby smiled, I will. Goodnight sweet princess."

"Goodnight Sir Toby." she called back as he walked out to the car.

Toby went home. He called Nancy the next day and they talked for hours.

CHAPTER 18

The Clunker, the Conflict, and the Pot Problem

Corey looked concerned as he gave Toby's new wheels the once over.

"Well. It's a car. And it's red." he said wrinkling his nose.

"I'll admit it's no GTX, but it doesn't drink near the gas that the GTX does." replied Toby. Corey went around the nineteen sixty four Ford Galaxy station wagon, kicking the tires. "What are you doing?"asked Toby.

"I don't know. I've seen my dad do this when he was looking at a car to buy." answered Corey.

"Think I'll pull the trailer with it this weekend. Me, you, and Fred can ride in comfort all the way there. I've even put an eight-track tape player in it so we can listen to tunes while kickin' back." said Toby.

The next Friday Toby went and picked up the trailer to haul the band equipment. He pulled up at Fred's house to load up.

Fred came out and said, "I kind of thought you might be pulling the trailer with the GTX."

"Nah. That thing drinks too much gas. And the throttle got stuck on it the other day. I was going down Broadway in front of Dixie Drug store and the next thing I knew, the second four barrel kicked in and I was up to eighty before I knew it. I don't think we want to go to Selma at the speed of light. So I thought I'd try out the old station wagon on this trip." answered Toby. "Is Birney gonna take his Sunbeam?"

Fred said, "Nope. He's gonna ride with Johnny."

Corey pulled up in his car and got out.

"Everybody ready for the next adventure?" Toby said, "Looks like we're going deep into redneck country. In the darkest realms of "the sticks."

They started loading the equipment into the trailer. Johnny and Birney showed up and started helping load the equipment. Toby was in the trailer packing the equipment when Birney came in the back toting a speaker cabinet. Toby sniffed in Birney's direction. "What is that smell on your clothes, Birney.?"

Birney smiled, "Oh. Johnny and me smoked a joint before we got here."

Toby blinked hard, "Since when did you start smoking pot?"

Birney said, "Johnny and I have been smokin' doobies for quite a while now. Why?" Toby was stunned. "This is the first I've heard of this." he said.

"Well don't worry Tobe. Johnny and me are gonna ride in his car." assured Birney.

"Man! Be careful. I'd hate to see you guys get busted. It's one thing getting caught with booze in your car, but pot? That's like saying "Hey, I wanna spend one to ten years in prison." worried Toby. "But then again. It's your life."

Birney frowned, "Whatever man. Look. Let's get this stuff loaded and go."

The band finished loading up and headed out for Camden, Alabama. It was a small town south of Selma, Alabama, on the

Alabama River. They had driven down to Clanton, when Toby noticed the temperature guage was climbing. He pulled over at a gas station, refilled the gas tank and checked the radiator, which was almost bone dry. He looked under the motor and noticed a puddle of water under it.

"Looks like I've got a leak in the water pump. No way to fix it with sealant, since it's the pump." he told Fred. "All I can do at this point is make sure there's water in the radiator." Corey piped up and said,"So what you're sayin' is, we'll have to check the gas occasionally and fill it up in the radiator."

Toby grinned, "Yeah. Something like that."

They filled up the radiator and went on to Camden. They made it to Camden city limits and stopped once again at a service station, where Toby found a couple of empty antifreeze jugs. He filled the radiator and the jugs, climbed back in and headed for the American Legion, where they were playing for a teen dance. The American Legion Post was located right next to the Alabama River. Birney and Johnny had stayed right behind Toby all the way to Camden. The two cars pulled up and parked in front of the building.

The guys set up and played their four sets. Several girls came up to Corey, flirting. A couple more cornered Fred and talked to him on breaks. A couple of local boys came up and grabbed one of the girls that was talking to Corey on break. One boy got in the girl's face yelling at her that she was nothing but trash.

Fred walked over and said, "Hey buddy. That's no way to treat a lady."

The boy turned and said, "You stay out of this big boy, or I'll fix your little red wagon.She ain't no lady. She's just trash that needs to be slapped around."

IT'S THE BASS PLAYER!

Corey said, "Does that mean you've got a taste for garbage?"

The boy looked at Corey with murder in his eyes and said, "You're gonna get yours smart ass! Let's step outside."

Just then two male chaperones walked over and grabbed the two boys by the arm and roughly escorted them to the front door.

"We've already called the cops, so if you boys will just hang around outside for a while, I'm sure they'll be happy to give you a ride down to the city jail." one of the chaperones said as they pushed the boys out the door.

One boy turned and yelled, "We'll be back to settle this!"

The chaperone said, "I don't think so." and went back inside.

The band finished playing and started packing up.

The girl with the irate boyfriend came over to Corey and said, "I'm sorry about Bobby Joe. He only gets like that when he's been drinkin'."

"Somebody needs to teach him how to treat a lady. You don't deserve his kind of crap." stated Corey.

"I know. But he's completely different when he's not drinkin'. Anyway, I thought I'd give you my phone number and address,so we can stay in touch. I like you Corey."

"Yeah. But you don't even know me." said Corey. "I could be as bad as him when I'm drinking."

"No. I don't think so. Besides, you've got an honest face."she said.

She handed Corey a piece of paper. Corey stuffed it in his pocket, got a pen and wrote his phone number and address on it, and gave it to her.

He said, "Well okay. So we can be pen pals or something."

She said, "I'd like that."

The band went outside and started packing the trailer. The chaperones stayed outside with them while they loaded up.

Toby had noticed a couple of cars parked at the gate entrance to the driveway for the American Legion, but thought nothing of it. They all got in their two cars and pulled off. They got down the road a small distance from the gate when Corey suggested they stop at the breakfast house in Selma and get a bite.

Toby said, "That's a good idea. But we need to tell Birney and Johnny what we're doin'". Toby pulled over on the dirt road. Corey hopped out and ran back to tell Johnny and Birney what they were going to do. A car came up behind Johnny's car and stopped. Corey was walking back to Toby's car when the jealous boyfriend came running up and grabbed Corey by the collar.

"I told you we'd settle this!" he growled.

He threw Corey up against Toby's car. Fred jerked his car door open and stepped up between Corey and his assailant. Fred stood a full head taller than the boy.

"You just made the wrong move!" sneered Fred.

Toby had gotten out and was coming around the car to help, when he noticed the boy had a friend who was walking up with a tire tool in his hand. He also noticed Johnny had gotten out of his car. He saw Johnny slip up behind the boy with the tire tool.

The boy standing there with Fred and Corey smiled, "Being big ain't gonna save your butt. I brought a friend with an equalizer."

Just then, Johnny, who was standing behind the boy with the tire tool, reached over and grabbed the tire tool out of the boy's hand. He then threw it across the road into the bushes.

Johnny said, "I'm your huckleberry. Pick on me."

The boy turned and took a swing at Johnny. It was the wrong thing to do. Johnny might have looked like a typical

IT'S THE BASS PLAYER!

hippy, with his long black hair and beard, with bell bottoms, but he was a black belt in Karate. He blocked the swing with a chop to the boy's wrist. He then made a round kick that landed in the boy's crotch. The boy doubled over. Johnny then swung with an open palm and hit the boy in the forehead while the boy was bent over. The boy went immediately over on his back, moaning, holding his crotch. Fred grabbed the other boy by the collars and said, "Okay tough guy. Your turn. Any last words before I pulverize ya?"

He drew back to punch the boy in the head.

"Just be glad it's me that's gonna whup ya, and not Corey there or Johnny. "Cause they're both black belts. Me? I just like to pound on people till they don't move no more."

The boy suddenly went from mad and menacing, to humble, scared and meek.

"Look. Maybe we got off on the wrong foot here. Hey man. I'm sorry if I bothered you! I didn't mean nothin' by it! Hey man. Please!"

Fred picked the boy up over his head like he was lifting weights, and flung him into the bushes with a loud, "WAAAAAAH!!!"

The boy slowly got up out of the bushes and limped back to his buddy's car. His buddy had gotten up slowly also and hobbled back to his car holding his crotch. Toby, Fred, Corey, and Johnny got back in their cars and left.

Fred asked Corey after they got back on the road, "You okay Corey?"

Corey replied, "Yeah. The only thing bruised is my ego. Thanks Fred."

"No problem my friend. We are the three muskyteers."

"I'll try not to ever make you mad, Fred. I wouldn't want to be turned into a human football." smiled Corey.

They drove to Selma and stopped at the breakfast house and ate breakfast. They talked about the skirmish and the upcoming Three Dog Night concert. Toby kept thinking about the pot smoking thing that was going on with Birney and Johnny. He didn't say anything that night on the way home. But he had made his mind up that he was going to say something to Fred about it the following week. Monday Toby called Fred and told him what he thought about Birney and Johnny's dope smoking.

"Well. If they're not doin' it when we're playin', then it's their business, Tobe. Not ours." observed Fred.

"I don't like it. What if we're goin somewhere to play a gig and they're riding with us and get busted. That means we could ALL get busted just for being in the car with them." countered Toby.

"Look. If it makes you feel any better, I'll make sure Birney and Johnny ride in a separate car from us. I mean. I'm not gonna fire 'em just because they smoked a little weed." offered Fred.

"I'm not asking you to fire them. I just want somebody besides just me to address this issue."

Fred said, "Tell you what. We'll have a band meeting Thursday night at the Place while we're setting up for the Friday night gig. How's that sound?"

Toby agreed, "Okay. But I don't want to be made the heavy in this."

"Awight. I'll see you Thursday Toby." answered Fred.

He hung up the phone and hoped the dope issue wouldn't blow up in his face.

Toby and Corey spent the day Tuesday cleaning and filling the Gable's pool. They had invited Nancy and Jane up to Corey's to go swimming on Wednesday, provided the pool was ready in time.

"Deja vue." said Corey as they filled the pool.

Toby turned to Corey and said, "What'd ya say Corey?"

Corey repeated, "Deja Vue. You know. Seems like we just did this same thing last year about this time."

Toby smiled, "Yeah. Come to think of it. It does seem like we've done this once or two million times before. Have y'all heard anything else from your neighbor, Brenda, since she ran away from her parents' house?"

"Nothin' yet. They know she moved in with some guy in Birmingham, but they don't know where and with whom. She's worrying her mom and dad to death. I mean. She's nineteen, but she's still a part of their family." answered Corey.

Corey's family and neighbors felt like an extension of Toby's own family. Whenever Toby felt down and needed somebody to cheer him up, he would always seek out one of the Gables. The next day, Toby went and picked up Nancy to go swimming at the Gables'. He picked her up in the GTX because his Ford station wagon was in the shop getting the water pump fixed. They pulled up at Corey's house. Toby got out and came around and opened Nancy's door for her.

When she stepped out, he said, "Wait. Wait. I forgot something."

Nancy looked puzzled and said, "What'd you forget?"

Toby slid his hands around her waste and said, "This."

He kissed her on the lips. She looked stunned for a second, and then put her arms around his neck and kissed him back.

They kissed for another ten minutes standing there, holding each other. Toby decided to stop before things got too far out of hand. He had a deep respect for Nancy and wouldn't do anything to disrespect her, like getting too carried away kissing her. After all, she was definitely a lady in his eyes.

"I like your compulsive kisses." she purred.

Toby smiled, "Never had my kisses described that way before. Come on. Let's go get wet."

They walked around to the pool to see Corey and Jane in the pool with water guns squirting each other. They took their tee shirts and shorts off, since they had worn their swimming clothes under their shorts and shirts.

"Got any more of those squirt guns Corey?" asked Toby as he and Nancy got in the water.

"Yeah. They're laying right there by the pool." answered Corey as he squirted Nancy. "All right! Don't start what you can't finish!" she said.

Nancy grabbed a water gun, stuck it under the water and filled it, then went on the attack, first squirting Corey, then Jane and then Toby. They all got their squirt guns and had a blast shooting each other. They swam and played in the pool all afternoon. They played chicken. Nancy on Toby's shoulders and Jane on Corey's shoulders. Nancy and Toby won the most rounds, knocking Jane off of Corey's shoulders more times.

Each time that Jane fell off Corey's shoulders, he would say, "Let me kiss your booboo." He would then kiss her on the lips.

"My lips don't hurt, but I like the booboo kisses though." she said.

Corey and Jane seemed like a natural match physically, as well as personality wise. Corey was six feet tall, skinny, with curly black hair, and Jane was about five feet ten, slightly thin, with dark brown hair. Toby and Nancy seemed like a good match too. Toby was five feet eight inches in height, stocky built, with dark brown hair and dark brown eyes, and Nancy was around five feet three inches, long blonde hair and beautiful brown eyes that always seemed to be smiling. After they got through playing in the pool, Toby and Nancy got dressed and

IT'S THE BASS PLAYER!

went by Toby's mom's house to introduce Nancy to his mom. Toby's mom, Louise, took an instant liking to Nancy. As Nancy took a liking of Toby's mom.

After they left, Nancy said, "Your mom is so cute! She's so little."

Toby smiled, "Yeah. One of her favorite sayings is "Dynamite comes in small packages". She might be small, but she can be feisty when she wants to be."

"Is that where you get your spunk from?" She asked.

"Well I reckon thar little lady." Toby smiled.

Nancy curled up to Toby's arm and said, "Thanks for letting me meet your mom. It means a lot to me."

"I'm glad you two hit it off so well." said Toby.

He turned and kissed her on the forehead. They were holding each other's hands to the point where they couldn't tell whose fingers were whose.

He thought, "I've finally found me a real classy lady who loves me as much as I can love her."

He carried Nancy home. When they pulled up in the driveway to her parents' house, Toby turned to Nancy, took a deep breath, and said, "I know we haven't been dating that long, but I feel we are connected in a very special way. And I would love for us to get closer. I know that I love you and you love me too, so I was wondering if you would wear my class ring."

He took his senior ring off his finger and put it in Nancy's hand. Nancy's mouth flew open.

"Oh Toby! I would love to wear your ring." she said as tears welled in her eyes.

She hugged Toby tight and kissed him. She then slid his senior ring on her finger. It was very loose on her petite hand, but she was very proud of it.

"I'll put some tape on it, so it won't fall off. Or, if it's allright with you, I may just get a necklace and wear it around my neck." she smiled.

Toby smiled back, "And that is one beautiful neck too."

He leaned over and kissed her on the side of her neck. They kissed for a while in the driveway at her parent's house and then he walked her to the door.

"Tomorrow. Same time. Same station, my love." he said as he held her at the doorway.

She kissed him on the cheek and said, "What's that?"

He said, "You know. I'll call you around the same time I always call you tomorrow." She giggled, "Oh. Okay. Same bat time. Same bat station then."

They kissed goodnight and Toby watched her go in the door. He heard her squeal with delight as she told her mother about the ring. He then walked out to his car, got back in, and left.

When he got home, he walked in the door and the phone was ringing. He went over and picked it up and said, "Hello."

Nancy's mom said, "Toby. This is Wilma, Nancy's mom. I just thought I would call you and tell you thank you for treating my daughter like a lady. Most boys these days are just after one thing, but you treat Nancy with the love and respect she deserves. She's a very good girl and I know you will always make sure she is treated like a lady. So I just thought I'd tell you thank you."

Toby blushed, "Shoot Mrs. Quebec, I would do anything for her. She is just what you said, a lady, and I will always treat her with the utmost respect. I've never had anyone treat me this good either. I hope we can all become very good friends. Your family and mine."

Mrs. Quebec said, "Well. I just thought I'd tell you that. Oh. We bought tickets to the concert in Birmingham that you boys are playing at, so we may see you there."

IT'S THE BASS PLAYER!

Toby smiled, "Hey. That'd be great Mrs. Quebec. Well, tell Mr. Quebec I said hello."

Wilma said, "I will. You have a good night Toby. Bye."

Toby hung up the phone and smiled from ear to ear. He felt complete.

CHAPTER 19

The Concert

Saturday, the big day of the concert had finally come. Everyone was excited to get to open for Three Dog Night. The concert was slated for Legion Field in Birmingham. Three Dog Night was just one of the big name bands playing there that night. Other bands, Like Rare Earth, Billy Preston, Steppenwolf, Tony Joe White, and Gilbert O'Sullivan were scheduled to play. Since the amplifiers, and P.A. equipment was already furnished, All the guys had to bring were their musical instruments, so they didn't have to rent a trailer for this gig. They loaded their guitars, Corey's drums, effect pedals, and Birney's organ into Johnny's van.

"Everybody ready?" called Fred as they got in the van.

"Ready to rock!" called Corey, as he gave a peace sign.

"All right! Let's do this thing!" called Toby.

Toby's mind was at ease about riding in Johnny's van with Johnny and Birney, since the band had a meeting the previous Thursday night. Fred addressed the pot smoking issue, and Johnny and Birney had agreed to leave their weed at home when they were on the road with the band. Toby and Corey had wanted to bring Nancy and Jane with them, but the band couldn't secure any backstage passes for anyone but the band.

"Looks like we finally hit the big time." said Corey excitedly.

Fred smiled, "Looks that way boys."

IT'S THE BASS PLAYER!

They drove up to the Legion Field parking lot and followed the signs to the area for the bands to park. There were five or six eighteen wheeler trucks with their trailers parked nearby. Fred handed everyone their backstage pass tags that he'd received in the mail.

He reminded the guys, "Don't lose these. If you do, you may find yourselves escorted to the parking lot."

The guys unloaded their instruments and took them to a secured area backstage. The guys mingled in with the other bands backstage. Fred went to find out when the Common Faith was supposed to go on.

The stage manager looked over the list and said, "Ah yes. Here you are. Wait a Minute. We've got two bands slated to play at the same time. You guys, the Common Faith, are slated to go on first, but there is a slash next to your band name that says Johnny Flash." Fred smiled, "Both those names are us. But we go by the Common Faith, so you can mark through the other name."

The stage manager made the change.

Toby had sat down next to a guy who looked very familiar, and started up a conversation.

"How's it goin'?" the man in sunglasses said.

"Hey. I'm Toby Martin. I'm the bass player for the Common Faith." Toby said as he stuck out his hand and shook the other man's hand.

"John Kay. I think you guys are on first. We're on about third or fourth. Have you eaten yet? They got some real good food over there if you're hungry."

"Not yet. Man! I cut my rock 'n' roll teeth on you guys and Hendrix. So where are you guys headed after you leave here?"

"I think our next gig is in Raleigh, North Carolina, doin' the same kinda show."

Toby chatted with John for quite a while. He learned that John had moved from Los Angeles to Nashville.

"Why would you leave L.A.? I mean. When you think of Steppenwolf, you think of Los Angeles." asked Toby.

"Well. L.A. ain't a safe place to bring up a family. Besides, I get a kick out of the yuckin' yayhoos in Nashville. Most of the people are friendly like a small town. They just don't know how to drive though."

Toby asked, "How many times have you had to change personnel in the band so far?" John smiled, "You sure you're not a reporter or somethin'? I dunno. Since we started out? Oh. Too many times to count. How bout your band?"

Toby grimaced, "Same story. People get into a band and realize they bit off more than they can chew. It's like the band keeps going through a constant metamorphosis. There's only three of us left that started this band."

John raised an eyebrow behind his sunglasses, "That's a big word, but it sounds like us too. Somebody's always comin' and goin'. All I can tell you is, keep doin' whatcha love. There'll probably come a time when the ones you love will want you to decide between the music you love and them. Women are bad about seeing your music as a competition instead of an extension of who you are."

Toby smiled, "Wow. That's pretty profound."

John got up and said, "Well. I'm gonna go chow down. You're welcome to join me. Oh yeah. Would you guys mind if I came out and jammed with you guys on stage on one of your songs?"

"Hey. I'm sure the guys wouldn't care." smiled Toby.

About that time, Fred came walking up and said,"Hey Tobe, we gotta go get a soundcheck. We're on first."

Toby said, "Yeah. I know. John just told me."

IT'S THE BASS PLAYER!

"Who was that guy you were talking to? He looked real familiar." asked Fred.

"Oh. That was John Kay. He's looking for a bass player." Toby said with a twinkle in his eye.

Fred's mouth dropped open. "You mean John Kay of Steppenwolf? Hey Tobe. You're not gonna leave me and Corey and break up the three muskyteers, are ya?"

Toby smiled, "Nah. I was just yankin' your chain, Fred."

Fred rounded up the rest of the band. Birney was swapping stories with Billy Preston. Corey was in a conversation with the drummer from Rare Earth. Johnny was talking to Mike Alsup, the guitarist for Three Dog Night. They went out on stage and started their sound check. The sound check lasted almost an hour. The sound engineer always tried to get the sound right with the opening act, so everyone else wouldn't have any problems. The guys ran over several tunes. Since this was a concert, They only played songs they wrote, instead of the usual cover tunes that they played in the clubs. When they finished the sound check, they went back stage again. The committee that had set up the concert had hired a caterer, complete with commercial sized barbeque grill. Everyone was sitting around eating and drinking, since it was a little after noon. Corey had piled his plate up with four large barbeque sandwiches, two bags of potatoe chips, and a large mess of baked beans.

Toby just shook his head and said, "I don't know where you put all that food Corey. If I ate that much, I'd be as big as the side of a house. I still don't know how you put away all those Stromboli steak sandwiches at Pasquale's that night you and Fred had the eating contest. I know Fred put away at least five whole sandwiches, but we lost count after seven with you."

Corey smiled between bites and said, "It's all in your metabolism Tobe. You know how I am. I can't hardly sit still anytime at all. Besides, I just pack it into my legs."

Toby snickered,"You said that. Not me."

At two o'clock, the guys were standing backstage with their guitars on their shoulders, ready to walk out and play when the announcer introduced them. Toby peeked around the curtain to see a sea of faces staring back at him. He figured there had to be over eight thousand people there. Fred, Johnny, and Toby did a last minute tuning of their guitars.

John Kay came up to Fred and said, "I take it you're the leader of this bunch of outlaws." Fred turned and shook John's hand. "It's an honor Mr. Kay."

"Please, just call me John. I was wonderin' if you guys would mind if I came out and jammed with you on that song, Thinking Thinking that you did at the sound check."

Fred said, "Bigger'n hell! Yeah. Definitely. We'd love it."

"All right. Well good luck guys."

Then they heard the announcer talking to the audience, getting them pumped up for the show. Then the announcer started the introduction of the first band.

"Ladies and gentleman, boys and girls, rockers and rocketts. Our first band is from right here in Alabama. How about a big hand for some of our home folks. Won't you please welcome The Common Faith!"

Corey and Toby took a deep breath and nervously said, "Well here we go."

They all ran out on stage to their positions behind their microphones and hooked up their instruments.

Fred hollered, "Hello Birmingham!"

Birney hollered over the roar of the crowd, "Let's rock this joint!"

"Our first song is called Gratitude, which is how we feel at this point for all you music lovers out there." yelled Fred.

IT'S THE BASS PLAYER!

Then Corey clicked off the first song. Toby looked out over the sea of faces and his knees almost turned to jelly. He looked down at his bass. Then he decided to close his eyes and do what he did best. After they played three songs, one behind the other, Fred said, "This next song will be on our next record that we will be recording soon. It's just plainly called "A Beautiful Song." The Common Faith played their tunes without flaw.

Toby thought, "This is where we should have been a long time ago."

When they started playing the song Thinking Thinking, John Kay walked out on stage and hooked up to an amplifier and started jamming with the band.

Fred hollered, "Ladies and gentlemen. Mr. John Kay!"

The crowd had been cheering while the band was playing, but when Fred introduced John Kay, the crowd went bonkers. John stayed out there with them through the rest of the show. As they finished their last tune, Toby wanted to keep playing, but he knew their part of the show was over. When they hit the last note, the crowd went crazy, giving the band a standing ovation.

Fred called out on his mic, "Thank you! Thank you! A special thanks to our new friend, Mr. John Kay."

They all took a bow and left the stage. They went and put up their instruments and stayed backstage.

John Kay came over to Toby and said, "Hey thanks for lettin' me jam with you guys. Anytime your band wants to open for us when we're in this area, you are really welcome."

Toby shook John's hand and said, "Thank you for making one of my dreams come true. To get to play on stage with you. I have one question though. That song, The Pusher. Did you ever have any troubles when you played that song? I know we played it a couple of times and had some really weird things happen afterwards. I don't know if it was coincidence, or if God was just telling us not to do that song."

John looked surprised and said, "Funny you should say that, because we've had some bad things happen after we played it too. We don't play it very often because of that very reason. Well, I'll talk to you some more later, my friend."

John left and went to his dressing room.

The band was standing around waiting for the next act to come on. The stage crews were busy rearranging the mics and equipment on stage for the next act.

One of the stage crew came up to Toby's band and said, "Which one of you guys is Toby Martin?"

Toby stepped up and said, "That would be me. What's up chief?"

"There's an insatiably beautiful blonde that wants to see you down at the end of the stage. I figure she must be kin or somethin' to ask for you by name." said the stage hand.

Toby followed the guy down off the end of the stage. There, standing with the biggest smile on her face, was that brown eyed, blonde haired beauty, Nancy. She and her cute friend, Sally were standing there. Toby came over and hugged her. She hugged him tight. It was a bigger thrill seeing Nancy there than it was playing the concert for Toby. The empty hole in his life was finally gone. He knew that what had been missing was Nancy. He had never been able to put a name on what he had missed until now.

"I am so proud of you." she said. "Mom and dad brought me so I could hear you play." "Well, I'm through playing, so I can sit out here with you, Sally, and your folks, and watch the rest of the show".smiled Toby.

"Mom and dad are very impressed with your band. And y'all got to jam with John Kay of Steppenwolf! Wow!" she said.

IT'S THE BASS PLAYER!

Sally beamed, "You guys were great at the prom, but y'all blew me away here! This is a Kodak moment. You mind if I take your's and Nancy's picture?"

Toby smiled, "Not at all."

Sally took several pictures of Toby and Sally, who could not seem to wipe the grins off their faces. It was obvious that they were definitely in love with each other and life itself.

Toby kept his stage pass on him while he sat with Nancy, Sally, and Nancy's parents, Mr. and Mrs. Quebec. When the last band was finishing up, Toby, Nancy, and Sally walked back down to the stage.

He kissed Nancy once more and said, "Thanks for coming."

"I wouldn't have missed it for the world." she said.

"I'll see you tomorrow pretty lady. I love you."

She said, "Okay. Be careful goin' home. Love you too."

They were having to yell in each others ear to hear each other because of the loud music and the noise from the crowd.

"You too sweet lips." said Toby.

He kissed her one more time and went back stage. Toby and his band hung around backstage for a while after the last band, Three Dog Night, finished playing. Most of the other band members were just plain down-to-earth folks like Toby and his band. After everybody started leaving, they loaded up their instruments, got in their vehicle and went home. Corey, Fred, and Toby couldn't sleep that night from being pumped up about the concert. Birney and Johnny went over to Birney's house and fired up some weed to celebrate. Many of the musicians that played that night went to parties afterward, where all kinds of drugs were available. Fred and Toby knew this, from the talk they heard at the concert. They knew Birney and Johnny couldn't go because they had to take the rest of the band home. Fred called Toby at two in the morning and they talked for an hour about the concert. When Toby hung up, he went to the bedroom and fell in his bed. Sleep found him in a matter of minutes.

CHAPTER 20

The Birthday Party

    Almost a week had gone by since the concert. The phones were ringing off the hook at Corey's, Fred's, and Toby's houses. With the exception of his conversations with Nancy, most all of Toby's conversations with friends and family were about the concert. These were conversations that he didn't start, but everyone else would. The local newspaper even had a segment about the local band playing with famous acts. The local radio station even called Fred up for an interview about the concert. The next day one of the radio stations in Birmingham called Fred and asked him and the guys to come on the radio station and present their record, as they would play one of their songs on the air that day. Fred and Toby had made sure and got the songs they wrote copyrighted, so if they ever got airplay, that Fred and Toby would get some kind of royalty checks from it. Fred had some forty five records made from the old tapes the band had made at Prestige studios, so the D.J. played their record that day. The entire week seemed to fly by.

    Toby woke up on that Friday morning after a good night's sleep. He was still thinking about the concert the weekend before. He smelled something good cooking in the kitchen. He got up and got dressed. He walked into the kitchen where his mother was cooking.

    "What's up mom?" he asked as he scratched his head and yawned.

"Oh. You were supposed to sleep late. Now get outa here. I'm baking a cake nosey." she smiled.

"Oh. Okay. I forgot today's my birthday." he smiled back.

Toby went and showered and shaved.

When he came out, his mom called out from the kitchen, "Tobe. I've got to run some errands this afternoon. You wanna ride with me?"

"Sure mom. I don't really have any plans today. Thought I'd pick up Nancy tonight and catch a flick." he said as he walked into the living room.

"Okay. I take it you like her a lot. Don't you? Cause I like her too. She's a very sweet girl."

"Yeah. She's pretty and cool." smiled Toby. "She's the first real lady I've met. I've been looking for a girl with some class for a long time. And her parents like me just as I am. No under currents of "you're not good enough for my daughter" junk going on in the background like the last girl I dated."

That afternoon Toby drove his mom to town to pick up some things. On the way back home, Louise asked him to take her by the Gables' house. As they pulled up in the driveway, he noticed a lot of cars there. They got out and walked up the driveway to the carport. They walked up to the door under the carport that went into the den, and knocked.

A voice inside said, "Come in."

Toby opened the door and stepped in.

A large crowd of people in the den hollered, "Surprise!"

Nancy came up and hugged Toby's neck and said, "Happy birthday sweety."

Toby turned red and said, "You guys! Y'all didn't have to do this!"

Everyone joined in on a round of happy birthday to you, as Gladys, Corey's mom, brought in the cake with the candles lit.

IT'S THE BASS PLAYER!

"Make a wish and blow em out Tobe." said Corey.

Toby made a wish and blew them out.

"Yay! Now let's get into that cake. You did a great job on it Mrs. Martin." smiled Corey. Corey's girlfriend, Jane, laughed, "You are definitely a bottomless pit when it comes to eating."

Corey just said, "Nah."

Mrs. Beige and her daughters, Paula and Brenda were there. Paula's husband, Harold didn't come, which was fine with Toby.

Mrs. Beige came over and hugged Toby's neck and said, "Well. I guess you boys didn't need my help after all to get your feet in the door to fame and fortune. I am so proud of all of you. And happy birthday Toby."

Toby smiled, "Thanks so much for coming. And thanks too for all your help with the Cowsill project we tried to get going."

Toby's brothers, Mark and Donald were there. Toby's friend, Billy French, who was home on leave from the Marines, came over and slapped him on the back and wished Toby a happy Cleepy birthday. Billy had enlisted in the Marines 6 months earlier and was scheduled to leave out for Vietnam soon. Ben and Pete Regis were there. Ben had gotten to come home on leave from the Army and came by. Pete had brought Joan with him. Even unpredictable Paul Thornton was there. Corey's brother John, and his girlfriend Karen were there. Even Donna Baddin came up and hugged Toby's neck and wished him a happy birthday. Nancy stepped up and put her arm around Toby's waste and smiled, "Sorry Donna, but he's taken."

Toby grinned and looked Nancy in the eye and said, "Yes I am. With you."

Mike Hammond had showed up with his wife Judy and their newest member to the family, Mike Jr. Don Frodo didn't come. He had moved away to Phenix City, Alabama. But his ex girlfriend, Denise had come to the party, to wish Toby a happy birthday from everybody at the store where Toby worked. Wanda, the piano teacher at the music store had made a huge Happy Birthday banner and had helped put it up on one wall of the den. Gwen McKelvey was there with her mom and dad to wish Toby a happy birthday. Gwen came over and hugged Toby's neck and wished him a happy birthday. Her mom and dad came over and shook Toby's hand, and said how proud they were that their daughter got to sing with such a nice bunch of boys.

Toby said, "It was an honor to have Gwen sing with us. She should try going professional singing. She would be great."

Nancy's best friend, Sally Killough was there with her boyfriend.

Sally said, "You two make the cutest couple Nancy. Toby, I think you two will go far. Happy birthday. We'll have to put on another party at mom and dad's house sometime soon like the one we had after the prom. I'll probably need some help cleaning up after the next party though. The last one I had to clean all the trash out of the pond by myself. And MAN! That was a chore. But the next time, you guys are gonna have to bring the music with ya. We'll set up a stage of some kind for you guys to play on."

Gladys came back in the den from the kitchen and said, "Toby. There's a phone call for you. It sounds like long distance."

Toby went in the kitchen and answered the phone.

"Hello. This is Toby Martin. Who is this?"

A familiar voice said, "Hello Toby. This is John Kay. I heard today is your birthday, and I just thought I'd call and wish you a happy birthday."

Toby was shocked and excited. "Hey John. Thanks for calling. Where are you at now?"

IT'S THE BASS PLAYER!

"We're in Illinois playing a gig tonight in some little bug tussle town. The guys wanted to play this song for you."

In the background Toby could hear Steppenwolf playing Happy Birthday Baby, as John sang on the phone."

While he was singing, Toby got Nancy to come over and listen.

"What is it?" she asked.

Toby beamed, "It's John Kay and Steppenwolf singing Happy Birthday Baby to me."

"You're kidding!" gasped a shocked Nancy.

The band finished playing and John came back on the line.

Toby said, "Man. I really appreciate you doing this. Who put you up to this anyway?"

John replied, "That football player guitar player of yours. He called me and said today was your birthday, so I thought I'd call. We'll be calling you guys soon to see about opening for us when we come back to Alabama. Happy birthday Tobe."

Toby smiled, "Thanks John. You take care and tell the guys thanks too."

John came back, "I will Tobe. See you soon."

Toby hung up the phone and just stood there smiling.

Corey came up and said, "Who was it Toby?"

Toby smiled, "John Kay of Steppenwolf and his band sang me happy birthday. He said he would be calling us soon to open for them here in Alabama when they come back through. And you can thank our guitar playing buddy Fred for this."

Corey piped up, "You're kidding! Wow! FAR OUT! Fred, if you was a woman, I'd hug your neck."

Fred just smiled and said, "Well I'm glad I'm not. I just thought I'd surprise you guys today."

Everybody started talking about the band opening for Steppenwolf excitedly. After the conversation died down about the new gig coming up, Toby got ready to open his presents.

Louise laughed, "Well Toby, How does it feel to be two decades old? My Lord! You're making me feel old now."

Toby smiled back, "Well mom. You're as old as you feel."

Birney Peters and Johnny Pate came in the door.

Birney said, "Sorry we're late. Did we miss anything? Anyway, happy birthday Tobe." Birney's brother, Tommy, came in behind Birney and Johnny. Toby came over to Tommy and shook his hand and told him he was glad to see him.

Birney smiled, "Well Tobe, we brought you a little birthday present that I think you might enjoy. Bring it in Motorhead!"

A guy named Motorhead, which was his nickname and not his real name, came in the door with a guitar case. Toby never knew why they called him Motorhead. His girlfriend, Julie Little came in behind Motorhead. Toby knew Motorhead and Julie from the Junior college that they all attended.

He said, "Tobe, I know a while back somebody stole your old Audition bass guitar, and you bought a Gibson to replace it, but we thought you might need a spare, just in case. So here you go."

Toby noticed that the case was for a Fender guitar.

Before he opened it he said, "How much do I owe you for this?"

Motorhead said, "Nothin. I have three Fender bass guitars. I don't need another one. This one is yours."

Toby was in shock. He just smiled and said, "You guys are the greatest! I don't know how to thank you enough."

Birney said, "Well open it up and see what it is."

Toby opened the case. Inside was a banana yellow nineteen sixty one Fender Telecaster bass guitar. Toby's mouth just hung open in awe.

I don't know if you've lost your mind Motorhead, but this is a classic. But I won't argue with it if you want to give it away."

IT'S THE BASS PLAYER!

Birney smiled, "This is from Johnny, Motorhead and me."

Toby shook Birney's, Johnny's and Motorhead's hands and thanked them over and over. Louise said to Toby, "You're dad would be proud of you if he could see you now Toby." Toby said, "I think he can see me from up there in Heaven. Thanks for making me who I am Mom. You've done a wonderful job raising us three boys since I was eleven. Like Mark and Donald said, you're our hero."

Nancy said, "And I especially want to thank you for bringing this ray of sunshine into my life."

Fred said, "Well. Enough of this sentimental horse pucky. Let's open some presents and go get into the pool."

Toby opened all of his presents. After he opened them all he thanked everyone. While he was thanking everybody, he noticed that Ben, Pete, Corey, John, and Birney had eased over behind Fred. They were all winking at each other, nodding at Fred behind his back, and grinning mischievously.

Ben said, "Hey Fred. Let's go get in the pool. Here. We'll help ya."

Pete, Corey, John, Ben, and Birney all grabbed Fred, picked him up, and toted him out to the swimming pool. Fred was struggling good naturedly, but to no avail. All the folks that were there followed the guys out to the pool. They toted him out to the edge of the pool and heaved him in. Ben was standing too close to the edge, lost his balance and fell in. As he fell, he grabbed Corey's and John's arms, at which they fell in with him. Luckily, Ben was wearing his fatigues and not his dress military uniform, so he didn't care if he got wet. Toby was standing there next to them. Tears running down his face from laughing so hard.

He turned to Nancy and said, "Oh why not?"

He turned and fell into the pool next to the other four guys. Then Nancy and everyone else started jumping in with their clothes on. Everyone except Toby's mother, who could not swim. After Donna fell in the pool, she came up out of the water and said, "Well. So much for that hairdo." She came over to Fred and said, "Fred. I hope you can forgive me for all the junk I put you through. I know you still care about me. I can see it in your face every time you look at me. If you want to, we can start all over again."

Fred smiled a wolfish grin and said, "Actually Donna, I don't feel that way about you anymore. I've found somebody who treats me good no matter what. Lorene doesn't see anybody but me when she walks in the room. She doesn't try to be the center of attention because she is the center of my attention. She doesn't have to, because my world revolves around her now. And we plan on getting married in the future. So you're a day late and a dollar short. And you know my motto. Think of the money."

Donna looked shocked and crushed.

Then she shook it off and said, "Well. There's always more fish in the sea, or pool, or whatever."

Brenda, one of the Gable's neighbors, came walking up to the pool from the driveway where she had just gotten out of a car that pulled off, and said, "Well Mrs. Gable, is this a private party, or can I join in too?"

Gladys turned and saw Brenda standing there and a look of shock came over her face. She said, "Oh. Brenda. You came home!"

Gladys got out of the pool and went over to where Brenda was standing.

Brenda simply said, "Yes ma'am. Mom and dad are so glad I wised up to what that jerk was doing to me. I am so glad to be home." Tears rolled down her face as she wept for joy. "I'm so sorry Mrs. Gable if I ever embarrassed you and your family."

IT'S THE BASS PLAYER!

Gladys simply said, "Oh. Don't worry about it hon. You're safe at home now. That's all that matters. I'm sure your folks are glad you're back. They love you so much and missed you."

Corey said, "Well Brenda. Since all the rest of us are already soaked, get in here with the rest of these crazy people!"

Brenda and Gladys both turned, walked over to the deep end of the pool and fell in, like a couple of winos. When they came back over to the shallow end, John, Karen, Corey, and Jane, Corey's girlfriend came over and welcomed Brenda home.

John waded over to Karen and said, "Hey. Since we're all jumping in here, I'd like to ask you to jump into something with me."

Karen looked suspiciously at John and said, "What's that?"

John pulled an engagement ring from his pocket and said, "Karen. Would you jump into marriage with me?"

Tears welled in Karen's eyes as she nodded her head and said, "Yes. Yes I'll marry you. You nut. But we're not getting married in the pool."

"Of course not. We'll get married on a boat in the Coosa River, then leave for our honeymoon on jet skis." teased John.

"Okay smarty. It'll be on dry land or nowhere." snickered Karen.

"No problem babe." answered John.

Toby said, "Well. This is the most off-kilter birthday party I've ever been to."

Nancy said, "And I'm just crazy about that crazy birthday boy." as she put her arms around his neck.

Toby looked at Nancy and said, "Better watch out. This proposal bug could get contagious. You never know who might propose next."

Jane looked at Corey and said, "Well…"

Corey just smiled and said, "Well don't look at me. I'm just the drummer. But you never know."

Nancy grinned from ear to ear and hugged Toby tight, as she sighed, "Oh Toby!"

Corey piped up, "Hey John. If y'all need music for the wedding, I know this really cool band that just opened for Three Dog Night."

Later that evening, everyone had gotten out of the pool and dried off. Gladys had to throw quite a few clothes in the dryer to get some of the folks' clothes dry enough to wear, since most of them didn't bring any extra clothes for the party. Toby and Nancy just dried off with a towel or two. They had worn their shorts and tee shirts, so there wasn't that much to dry off. Toby looked at Nancy and thought how cute she looked with her towel wrapped around her head.

Louise said, "Toby. If you don't stop holding Nancy's hand so much, you're going to cut the circulation off. She's not going to run away from you."

Toby smiled, "I can't help it mom. She's like my better half." He smiled at Nancy and said, "She makes me complete."

Nancy smiled and kissed Toby on the cheek and said, "I feel the same way about you Tobe. In all my seventeen years, I've never had anybody treat me this good and care so much about me. No fussin', no fighin'. Just lots of love from this sweet man."

Fred just rolled his eyes and said, "There goes the romantic flood again."

Fred and Corey had brought all the band equipment to Corey's house and put it in the building next to the pool. Everything was set up for a jam session. That evening there was a super jam session at the Gable's house. Everybody took turns playing music with everybody else. There were plenty

IT'S THE BASS PLAYER!

of vocalists, guitar players, keyboard players, and one other bass player, so Toby swapped out playing with everybody else that jammed that day with Motorhead, who was the other bass player. Toby played on his new Fender bass guitar. At one point, Donna and Gwen were singing a duet. Corey bragged about how awesome they sounded together. And everyone sang together on everything that was played. The last song they played that evening was "So Happy Together" by the Turtles. On the last two choruses, the music stopped and everybody sang without accompaniment. At one point, Toby got down on one knee and sang the chorus to Nancy while holding her hand.

Corey had gotten off the drum set about halfway through the last song and gave the sticks to his brother John, who could also play. John sat down behind the drums and started playing.

Corey took Jane by the hand outside to the patio and said, "Shall we dance Lady Jane?" Corey then bowed and Jane curtseyed to him. He took her hand and assumed a waltz position.

Jane smiled, "I would love to, Sir Corey."

Sir Corey and Lady Jane started waltzing around the patio outside while everyone was singing the last song.

Gladys beamed, "That's my boy."

> The End.
> (or is it?)

Would you like to see your manuscript become a book?

If you are interested in becoming a PublishAmerica author, please submit your manuscript for possible publication to us at:

acquisitions@publishamerica.com

You may also mail in your manuscript to:

**PublishAmerica
PO Box 151
Frederick, MD 21705**

www.publishamerica.com

CPSIA information can be obtained at www.ICGtesting.com
234695LV00001B/51/P